Lover Girl

Lover Girl

A NOVEL BY

NICOLE SELLEW

Chapter One

"I want you to feel at home here," he says. I stare at the refrigerator and think about how much easier everything would be if I didn't still want to sleep with him. He pulls a carton of orange juice out of the fridge and then closes the door just as it starts to make the tinny beeping noise that means it's been left open for too long.

There's a humming silence. Enough time passes, and I have to say something now. "Yeah, of course."

He starts rolling another joint and his big knuckles make his fingers look like insect legs, which does not sound sexy but is, completely and irresistibly.

"Do you, um, do you know when you're going back to the city?"

"Tomorrow morning," he says, taking a break from rolling to look up at me. When he makes eye contact he makes it unblinkingly. My body moves toward his.

"Oh," I say.

"I know." He offers me the carton of orange juice and I wave my hand to reject it, because I know the sugar in it will make my mouth taste bad and I'm still holding out hope that he'll kiss me soon. "Some bullshit opening tomorrow. And then I have to fly to Phoenix." He licks the paper and I can see the space between his tongue and his lips. I almost shudder with how badly I want him but manage to keep rigidly still, so still that my back is starting to hurt from being unsupported on the white barstools. "Let's...go outside and smoke this."

I thought he might have been about to say something else and I stare up at him, frowning, and he goes, "what, did you want to smoke inside?" and I just laugh and shake my head and stand up so that he can't see my eyes.

We walk out front where there's a bench that overlooks some bird feeders. There's no bird food in them now, but Lucas says I should buy some and put it in there while I'm here. He thinks watching the birds will be good for my creativity. I don't tell him that I'm afraid of birds, I just say I'll do it.

Lucas lights up and then we smoke a little bit and I worry that now we'll have nothing to say to each other.

"It's really pretty here," I say, and he takes another long drag.

"Is it wrong that I don't think so?" he asks flatly after he exhales, and then he gives a half-cough, half-laugh.

"Why not?"

"I don't know," he says. "I grew up coming here, so maybe I'm desensitized to it." When he passes me the joint our hands touch and his feel extremely cool and dry, which makes me self-conscious about how warm and damp mine are. Even though I know I'm too pretty for him I constantly feel like he's way too important and wealthy to be interested in me sexually. "But it's like, objectively nice here." I make to give him the joint back and he parts his lips a little, meaning he wants me to put it in his mouth with my fingers, which is obviously a sexy thing to be doing. I do it and he nods a thank you and then we sit quietly, him smoking and staring into space and me craning my neck to look at the stars.

"Do you miss your parents?" I ask, because I know they've been in London for six months and he hasn't seen them.

"No, not at all," he says. "We're not close."

I know a little bit about his parents and I want to seem interested but I also don't want to pry. If I ask too many questions I'll be one of those annoying girls who just wants to hang out with him because he has rich parents, or maybe I'm just high now and overthinking something that could be very simple.

"Do you want to swim?" I ask, and then we both giggle.

"Yeah," he says. "Yeah, I guess."

"You guess?"

"Yeah, I guess." I giggle again and then get up and walk around toward the side of the house, where a wooden gate leads to the back garden and the pool—I remember from the tour that Lucas gave me when I got in this morning, and from when I was here years ago. I stand by one of the lounge chairs and slowly take off my clothes until I'm naked and shivering.

"It might be too cold for this," I say. Lucas is looking at me now, and I see desire in his gaze for the first time since we slept together in New York. I guess all it took was me getting literally naked in front of him.

"It's not too cold," he says, and then he undresses next to another lounge chair. I try not to stare at him with obvious lust and it can't be done so I walk over to the pool and down onto the second step so that the top half of my thighs is submerged.

I stand there shaking and he comes over and splashes past me and into the pool. He shakes his wet hair off his forehead after he dunks and the droplets splatter onto my naked chest, my face, my throat. I shriek and laugh and then he pops up and grabs my forearm and pulls me into the water with him. Our bodies brush past each other slimily but it doesn't really feel like it counts as touching. I open my eyes underwater even though they burn and I look at his skin until it hurts too much and I have to poke my head out, gasping and spluttering.

I twist away from him and swim to the deep end—it's not an Olympic pool, or even a 25-meter one, but it's quiet and still when I get over here; the ripples from Lucas' movement don't reach me.

It's dead silent except for crickets and frogs and the sound of Lucas panting. He's floating on his back and starts to lazily do the elementary backstroke over to me. I say, "chicken, airplane, soldier," and he says, "what?" and I tell him I learned how to do that stroke when I was a little kid at swim practice.

"I thought I was doing dead man's float," he says, and now he's flipped onto his front to tread water and look at me.

"That's if you're not moving," I say. "It's what you're supposed to do if you're stranded at sea."

He doesn't say anything for a while, just swims closer to me and flips over again. I can feel his ripples now, and it's almost like he's touching me. "If I were lost at sea," he says, still on his back and looking up at the stars, "and only you knew where I was, would you rescue me?"

"I don't know." I look at him and then follow his gaze to the sky. I don't know anything about constellations because I'm afraid of space and science, but I bet Lucas does. He seems like he would know the Big Dipper, at least. "Maybe. Yeah, I guess I would."

"What?" He flips over and starts treading water again, close enough to me now that I can feel his legs brushing past mine. "I would do it for you. In a heartbeat." His voice is genuinely wounded but his eyes are flat and cold like always, reflecting the clear surface of the water.

"I believe you," I say. Our faces are close now, and I can feel the heat from his breath. He's breathing hard, either because he's treading so much water or because he's a smoker. I'm breathing hard too, though, and I don't smoke. I wonder if he feels the warmth of my breath and if he thinks it feels good. We're both naked and so close to touching and I think he kind of just told me he loved me in his own twisted way and it smells like hydrangeas and jasmine—and yet there's nothing romantic about the situation at all. I feel stoned and happy, like my skin is butter and the water is silk, but it's still like being alone even though Lucas is right here. He looks at me but I think he only sees the flowers and the high gate around the backyard reflected in my eyes. Which is fine. Some people are just like that.

"Race you," he says, and then he swims to the shallow end and climbs up the stairs and over to the lounge chair and his clothes. I follow him, breathing hard and confused by what's happening, if anything's really happening at all.

* * *

When I graduated college I thought I would be famous. Or at least successful and happy, living in New York or Europe or somewhere equally glamorous. Hong Kong, maybe. I thought I would have a job at a magazine or something vague and amorphous, like girls who "work in fashion" or are "creative directors."

"When did you stop thinking that?" Lucas asks, and I realize I'm speaking out loud.

We're in bed now, staring at each other, our faces inches apart. His breath smells like spliff and orange juice and peanut butter. It's delicious. My left leg is between both of his and he's softly trailing his fingers up and down the inner part of my arm. When he reaches the crook of my elbow my breath catches a little bit, but I can't tell if he notices. If he does he ignores it.

"I guess I still think that," I say. "That's why it's so strange that this is really my life."

He reaches up to me and brushes a piece of my hair away from my face. Our eyes are locked and his are such a cold and pretty blue (my dad's eyes are also this color) and I say, "you're important to me, Lucas. Um, in my life." Then he closes his eyes and doesn't say anything, and almost instantly his breathing becomes slower and deeper, and within thirty seconds he twitches and I know he's asleep. And I wish I hadn't said anything.

My hair is still wet and I think about how I was going to suggest a shower but then Lucas fell asleep. It's not terribly late, just past two maybe. And Lucas usually stays up all night. Maybe he feels safe enough with me to fall asleep without thinking about it. Or he was just tired.

* * *

It really is the strangest thing how I came to be here; and yet it happened so naturally that it almost would have seemed absurd if I'd ended up anywhere else.

I saw Lucas in the city in August and we got drunk together and I told him I didn't know what I was doing with my life, and he asked me if I was still writing. I said yes, I'm working on a novel, and he said I should stay at his parent's beach house and finish it, because they're not going to be there and I can just be the caretaker or something until they get back from Europe and New York and wherever else they'll be. So I quit my job at the pizza place near my parents' house and moved into Lucas' three weeks later.

Because Lucas and I sleep together sometimes I thought it might make me feel bad and strange to live in his family's house, but it doesn't at all. It feels pretty normal, I guess because I never cash in on being a pretty girl otherwise—like I don't let people buy me drinks at the bar, and things like that.

My parents didn't really care, either. They said it sounded like a nice idea and that maybe they'd come visit if they weren't too busy later in the fall. I think they were just happy to have me out of the house and doing something other than waitressing. I worry that they think they wasted all that money on my fancy liberal arts college, but I also think it's kind of too late. When you're a smart girl you're kind of expected to get a liberal arts degree and then be depressed and aimless for a while. That or work in publishing.

* * *

When I wake up in the morning Lucas is gone, which is surprising because I'm usually a light sleeper, so I thought I would have heard him leave. I check my phone and he texted me two hours ago that he didn't want to wake me up and he'll see me soon. That's that, I guess.

Lucas has to go back to the city and then to Phoenix because the fake job his mom got him at some art gallery requires him to work three days a week, sometimes, or to travel around and buy art. It's all so vague to me but I imagine he has a pretty great time smoking cigarettes and talking to other rich people.

I get out of bed and make a smoothie with frozen fruit that's been in the freezer for a really long time, probably, and then I eat Lucas' leftover ham sandwich from the deli yesterday. I don't know why he didn't take it back to the city. Maybe he thought of me when he was leaving, and knew I wouldn't be very capable of feeding myself. That or he forgot about it.

Lucas' house is all windows, so I can see the pool out back and the hedges and fence around the perimeter. The hedges are tall enough so that no one would ever be able to see me, but the windows make me feel like I'm constantly exposed. The sun streams in, at least, and all the white and chrome and everything in here sparkles and it's so clean and beautiful that it almost makes me feel clean and beautiful too.

I don't want to be out front by the bird feeders, because that will remind me of last night's conversation with Lucas, so I take the smoothie out by the pool and FaceTime a friend. She doesn't pick up, so I try a few other people. Nell answers—my Chicago friend—and she's wearing sunglasses and sitting on some horrible Midwestern beach where the sand looks dirty. Not that the beaches aren't choked with seaweed and trash here, but still. At least it's not the Midwest.

"You look like shit," she says. I tell her I was up late with Lucas. "Did you guys fuck?" she asks, and I tell her we didn't. She wrinkles her nose and I say, "I know," and then she blinks through her sunglasses and I can tell she's looking at her own face in the corner of the screen. Nell says the place looks nice and that maybe she'll come visit for a long weekend.

"It's all so strange and terrible," I say, and she laughs.

"It sounds like fun."

"Yeah. It is, I guess."

I look at the pool which is sparkling and inviting. The smoothie I made tastes like vanilla for some reason and I should be happy but I'm not, not at all, and I don't know why.

"Are you doing a lot of writing?" Nell asks, and I tell her I am even though I'm not. I think I need to have sex before I can write. Sometimes that's a feeling I get, like I'm blocked up and need someone to jostle the ideas free, and sex is the only way I know how. But I worry if I tell that to Nell then she'll think I'm crazy.

"How's Chicago?" I ask, and Nell launches into a story about a guy with a neck tattoo who bought her and a friend bottle service at the club. She says she slept with a musician she met online and it was not that good and now she's bored. "I'm bored too," I say, and she tilts her head back and laughs.

"Go out and find some hot people," she says. "You're in the right place for it." We talk a little bit about a mutual friend of ours who is crazy and living in New York now and then I hang up and kick at the mulch on the ground by the hydrangeas. Some of the petals are tipped with brown and curling in on themselves, but some are still late-summer powder blue, and it makes my chest hurt because all I can think about is it being summer and me being happy. But unless I want to hibernate or move to Hawaii I have to figure out how to be happy now, when it's getting colder and darker every day.

I go back into Lucas' kitchen and regret hanging up with Nell, even though our conversation depressed me and made me not want to talk to anyone. I wash out my smoothie glass and stare at the strip of white wall between the sink and the window and get the sense that my life could very easily become boring and meaningless if I'm not careful.

* * *

I'm not a huge slut, not really. When I was packing for Lucas' I felt like Haydée from that Éric Rohmer movie. *La Collectioneuse*. But I'm not as thin as she is and I don't collect men. I just like sex and find that when I'm not having it regularly I get ennui. I'm not like some of my pretty friends who use sex as a tool to get things and I'm also not the kind of girl that men go crazy for. Usually they seem to keep me at a very appropriate emotional distance, and I've always wondered whether this is because it's what they want or because they think that's what I want. Could be a bit of both—but I never ask, so I never know. Plus you can never really trust anything people say, boys especially.

Lucas is my high school friend but we didn't start sleeping together until college, when I saw him in the city completely at random and he invited me over to smoke and brought me out here, actually. I think he forgot about that, though. The bringing me out here, not the fact that we've had sex. Anyway. He said he'd always kind of wanted to sleep with me and I said I'd always wanted to sleep with him too. At a grad week party in high school we'd told each other that if we were still single at thirty we'd get married, which at the time felt like a big deal but is really just something people drunkenly say to each other.

I slept with people in college—not as few as some and not as many as others. I had a boyfriend for a long time because when you're a girl having a boyfriend legitimizes your existence. But when you're single you can have your existence legitimized all over town, I'm finding.

After Lucas and I slept together he asked if we were best friends now and then we both laughed. I think he might have been serious, though. The more time I spend with him the more I realize that he doesn't have very many friends.

Lucas

Half a bar when I'm through security. This is a prescription, but I have other drugs in my backpack, shoved between the pages of a book some girl gave me. I forget the girl. I forget the name of the book.

Another half when I'm on the plane. And now I don't have to think about anything.

When we land, it's sunny. I think about taking another half, but it's better to save it. I forget where I am, where I'm coming from. The vague sense that I'm forgetting something else, something important. But that goes away quickly. The air is hot. I step off the plane into the desert. I blink into the sun. Why am I here? I don't have to remember—I never do. Someone is already here, waiting for me, my name in black marker on a white sign.

Chapter Two

The days go by quickly here and I can take naps for the first time in my entire life. It's been a week since Lucas left and I've left the house four times: twice to go grocery shopping, once to go to the beach, and once just now, to buy a sandwich from a café because I waited to eat until four PM and started to feel like I was going to pass out.

The sandwich I bought is pesto mozzarella and tomato. When I ordered it I pronounced mozzarella like "mozarelle." It cost sixteen dollars but it doesn't really matter because my parents are giving me money for food. I thought it would be difficult to accept money from people when I stopped being a student, but it's very easy. All I have to do is say I need money and not think too hard about the fact that I'm stealing someone else's time from them. The sandwich tastes like nothing, but I feel better once it's in my stomach.

After I take a few bites of the sandwich I settle on four different photos for my Tinder profile: one where I'm pouting, one with a friend (so I don't seem like an insane loner), one where I'm smiling next to a dog (so I seem nice and normal), and one where my body looks good (this for the obvious reason). I create the profile and think about how easy it was to just become a person who does this now. My sandwich is dripping and I shamelessly lick the cheese grease from my fingertips. There's still a bit until sunset and the blue of Lucas' pool is deep and glittering, and I think about how maybe when I'm done with the sandwich I'll strip down and take a dip to get rid of all the grease. It's warm and with my eyes closed it feels like summer.

I shovel the last wet bit of sandwich bread into my mouth and then peel off my shirt (the same shirt I've been wearing for three days) and my pants (fresh jeans that I put on to go to the café) and then I'm naked (no bra or underwear). I imagine that someone is watching me through the gaps in the hedges, and that's what makes me feel beautiful. Without an imagined gaze, I am not real.

Because it's the Hamptons I kind of assumed everyone on Tinder here would be rich and clean and hot, but actually there's a lot of ugly people. Within five minutes of swiping someone has already asked me to get drinks and three people have complimented my physical appearance. So I guess I get it now. It's something with the algorithms, I'm sure, but the way the screen lights up every time I get a match gives me a physical dopamine rush. I have the feeling that I'm going to become very addicted to this. While I'm trapped here, behind the hedges, the internet is the only physical place where people desire me.

When I finish swiping I tuck my phone between my discarded clothes and get in the pool. Lucas' family heats it, of course, but he told me not to heat it unless he tells me to, which he hasn't. It's refreshingly cool and salty like the sea—I think it's the first saltwater pool that I've ever been in. When I swam with Lucas the other night I didn't notice the salt at all, probably because I was too busy wondering if he was going to fuck me.

Under the water everything is quiet except for the sound of blood rushing in my ears. I open my eyes and the salt stings but I leave them open and look at the blurry outline of my hands and the floating chunks of my hair. I feel like a mermaid, except a mermaid wouldn't be alone like this. Someone would be watching her.

When I get out of the pool I check my phone dripping wet and the little droplets of water that splash on it magnify the pixels.

There are boys from online who want to see me and I stand in Lucas' backyard naked and panting from my swim, debating whether it would be a breach of some unspoken code if I started going on Tinder dates while staying in this house.

The wind changes. I shiver. I feel the conviction that someone or something is concealed in the hedges, watching me, but when I move closer, the wind has stopped and I feel silly.

The air is completely still, now, and steamy with September heat. I decide that I'll meet up with a bassist for a drink.

When I get out of the shower he's already decided on a bar and a time. It's all very easy for me. I think about wearing a dress but I don't want to seem like I'm trying too hard, so I put on baggy jeans and a tight pink tank top that stretches so thin over my tits that my nipples are completely visible. My desire to appeal sexually viable outweighs my self-consciousness about my nipples, so I decide not to change.

I have my mom's shitty Honda, so I could drive into town, but Lucas' house is only like a mile away and I have forty-five minutes until I need to meet the bassist. It makes sense to walk so I put on my chunkiest sneakers and slip out the door. Lucas said to lock it when I go out but I think that's stupid so I don't, I just shut the door and assume that because my car's in the driveway no one will break in. Probably this is dumb of me but I can't be bothered to care, not when Lucas so clearly doesn't.

* * *

I walk past the bar because I know I'm early, and the bassist has already messaged me to say he's running late. I decide I'll do a lap around town to try to orient myself. It's a strange place and I'm starting to see why Lucas doesn't necessarily think it's pretty.

The restaurants glow warm and golden and their tables —full of beautiful people—spill out onto the sidewalk. Everyone sitting and eating is young or thin or both and it makes me feel like I'll probably never go out to eat here. There's a gelato shop and a blonde mom is yelling at a toddler in a Ralph Lauren polo shirt to stop crying, which is only making him cry more. He doesn't have any gelato and I wonder if that's why he's crying.

I slip into an alleyway and wander back into a tiny courtyard lit by fairy lights where I think they sell coffee during the day. Right now the little coffee stand is shut down, but there are cushioned benches and those thick-leaved plants with waxy tips that always look fake to me. I sit on the bench and think about how it would be very romantic to be here with another person. There's something romantic about being here alone as well but it's mostly just quiet. I check my phone and Tinder guy says he's trying to grab us a table and there's no time to have any more profound thoughts because here I am with the ultimate distraction: someone who will potentially have sex with me. I feel heat in my stomach and wonder if I should just go back to Lucas' and sleep and sleep and never get out of bed again.

Be right there, I type. I wish I had worn a jacket, because now I'm painfully aware of my nipples, but I'm sure it'll be dark enough in the bar for them to seem charming and alluring rather than abjectly prominent. Besides, it's a warm night, an Indian Summer, even though I don't think you're supposed to say Indian Summer anymore.

The bar has a blue awning and no outdoor seating and when I walk in it's more crowded than it looked from the outside. The boy is looking around and obviously waiting for me and I give him a hug and introduce myself and I wonder if the people around us can tell we're on a weird first internet date but then I remember that nobody cares and also everyone does this now.

"Do you want a drink?" he asks, and I nod because even though I don't particularly want a drink we're at a bar and I kind of feel like I have to get one or I risk seeming weird, or worse, not chill. He leans against the bar and even though he's a bit awkward I'm still attracted to him. I don't think we'll have sex but that's always my first feeling with someone so maybe we will. He asks what I want to drink and I panic and can't think of anything to say except "vodka tonic" which is perhaps one of my least favorite drinks ever. He orders me a vodka tonic and I think about offering to pay but I also feel mute and still like a beautiful stone statue of a wood nymph but with giant ugly nipples.

"Let's get a table," he says and hands me my drink. It was easy to let him pay. I immediately take a sip of it and it tastes like straight vodka without even the suggestion of tonic. I wonder if he was really trying to get a table when he texted me earlier that he was or if that's just something people say they're doing when they're the first person at the date.

We sit in a corner that's lit solely by one of those fake

candles with the plastic flame that waves electronically back and forth like real fire.

"What did you get?" I ask, and he says, "same as you," so I lean my glass in and give his an ironic clink. "It's bad luck to do that if your drinks are different," I say.

He looks at me blankly, a doltish half-smile on his face. "What," he says. I shake my head like never mind and prepare myself for what will undoubtedly be a grueling experience. People say you decide whether you want to sleep with someone within five seconds of meeting them (and I do want to sleep with him) but I think it also takes five seconds to decide whether you can speak to someone without wanting to blow your brains out.

My back is pressed against the dark wood of the wall and I'm looking half at this boy and half at the rest of the bar, which is mostly full of people much older or younger than us.

"I feel like there's a lot of underage kids here," I say, and he nods and takes a big sip of his drink before saying, "oh yeah, I came here all the time in high school." I frown because I can't tell if he's joking. My drink is almost half gone. Or there's still half a drink left, if I were the type of person who thought about things in that way.

I ask the bassist what he's doing here and where he went to college and other questions of this nature and almost immediately I can't hear anything he's saying so I settle into the pattern of widening my eyes and then nodding based on the general cadence of his sentences. After about five more minutes I can kind of tell more seriously that we're not going to fuck. He says he has to go somewhere later tonight for a gig and he doesn't invite me or even tell me where it is which is definitely indicative of his lack of sexual interest in me and therefore in my lack of worth as a person. I wonder if he decided he didn't want to in the first five seconds or if it took him longer than that.

We do keep drinking, though, mostly because he keeps offering to buy me drinks, and I think that maybe it's time to start saying yes to things like this. Finally the fourth round I say I'll buy and when I stand up to go to the bar I have to grab the table because everything tilts rapidly to the side. I smile and hope I seem charming and coquettish rather than ungainly and drunk. While I wait at the bar I cross my arms so my nipples are covered. I'm so drunk that everyone kind of seems like an NPC to me and I start laughing to myself a little bit while I lean on the bar and try to get the (ugly) bartender's attention. He comes over eventually and the second I take my arms away from my chest he starts staring at it. I order two double gin and tonics because it's what feels right and then I have to pay twenty-two dollars in cash for them. I give twenty-five and tell the bartender to keep the change. He looks at me strangely and I give him a half-salute that I hope doesn't look too Hitlerian and then spillingly carry the drinks back to the table.

"I have to go soon," says the bassist. His eyes are bluish-grey, not pure blue like Lucas', and I smile blankly and vacantly. "Okay," I say. "That's right." Even while I talk I don't let the sweet girl smile melt off my face. I feel like a little kid pretending to be an adult.

The bassist starts talking about how much he likes to go bird-watching and how great it is to bird-watch out here. I nod and then interrupt him in the middle of a sentence to say that I'm deathly afraid of birds. The r's feel thick in my mouth and he stares at me like I have three eyes. He gives no indication that this piece of information is charming or interesting. His eyes look even greyer now, like approaching storm clouds. It feels like a bad omen. Or maybe I'm just drunk.

Eventually he says he'd better get going and I nod dumbly and then we stand up. We walk toward the exit and he says he's going to go to the bathroom, to which I say nothing. I give him a slack-mouthed drunken stare and he slips into the bathroom and I stumble into the night air which is as cool and bracing as night air usually is. It's a clear enough evening that I can see some stars and it makes me ache inside my chest. I mumble "why," and realize that I'm good and proper drunk, maybe to the point where I shouldn't walk home, but I don't think they have Uber here and anyway I don't have the app downloaded on my phone. I didn't say goodbye to the bassist but I think that's the sexy and mysterious choice.

While I walk I rake my palms across the spiny hedges that hide people's houses and think about how I kind of wish my date was a DJ or something because then he would have at least been easier to make fun of.

* * *

I push in the front door and immediately I can tell something's wrong. The lights in the kitchen are on and music is playing faintly. For a second I think Lucas might be back—but it's A$AP Rocky, which Lucas would never play.

I'm too drunk to be afraid so I take off my shoes slowly and wait for whoever is here to come out and kill me. It does kind of look like Paul Allen's apartment from *American Psycho* in here with all the white furniture and rich people tchotchkes, so it would only make sense that someone would get axe-murdered in here and that the someone would be me.

The toilet flushes and then a boy I know comes out of the bathroom, completely naked.

"Hey, Cameron," I say.

"Oh shit," he says. "That's right. You live here now." He makes no move to cover himself.

I smile and then start to giggle a little bit. I worry I seem really drunk but I'm so drunk that the worrying stops fairly quickly, and then he's giggling too. "I'd give you a hug," I say, then I trail off and gesture to his naked body.

"Yeah," he says, and then we both start laughing again.

"What the fuck are you doing here?" I ask.

He shrugs. "I'm on vacation."

"In September?"

"I'm taking time off school."

"Oh." I could ask him why he's taking time off but he probably doesn't want to talk about it while standing naked in the kitchen. Then I say, "you're dripping," and motion toward the glimmering puddle of water that's accumulating on the white marble by his feet. "Somebody'll crack their head open." He looks down haplessly but doesn't seem like he's going to move and I say, "me, probably."

He snorts and then walks toward the bathroom while I throw myself down on the couch near the door. "What the fuck were you doing out so late?" he shouts from the bathroom, and then he emerges with a towel around his waist. "Don't you like to go to bed early?"

His hair is longer than the last time I saw him but his mannerisms are the same, like he just had a growth spurt and doesn't know how to handle the newfound length of his limbs.

"Usually," I say. "But I sleep all the time here."

"Yeah, dude," he says. "It's such a sleepy place."

"Did you just call me dude?" I ask at the same time that he asks, "are you drunk?" and then we both laugh again.

He sits in the loveseat catty-corner to the couch I'm on and I make a big show of peeling off my socks very sultrily. I remember that I didn't lock the door and I guess I'm lucky it's only Cameron and not an axe murderer, but it would have been kind of nice to get chopped in the back of the head so hard that I never had to worry about anything ever again.

"Yeah," I sigh once I've finished taking off my socks, "I'm drunk." I don't know why I took my socks off but now I put my feet up on Lucas' glass coffee table next to the stone statue of some strange, unidentifiable animal and wiggle my toes and laugh. "Did you know I have flat feet?" I ask.

"You *are* drunk," Cameron says. He makes unblinking eye contact, just like Lucas. The effect is especially disconcerting with Cameron because his eyes are such a dark brown that the iris and pupil blend together when he's far away like he is now. When we used to lie in bed together the sun would come in and shoot through the brown of his irises in golden streams like tiger's eye. But now, in the low indoor light, his eyes look pure black.

"Are you hungry?" he asks, and I nod. I realize that I'm starving. I haven't eaten since that greasy sandwich, which is the only thing I've eaten in almost forty-eight hours. It makes me feel very powerful and skinny but also like I could eat.

"I'm so hungry," I say, and then I laugh and he laughs too.

Cameron goes to the kitchen and starts opening cupboards. He never cleaned up his puddle of water, and I stare at its edges, which bubble up slightly from the smoothness of the marble. "What the fuck is this?" Cameron says, holding up a plastic bin of pine nuts from the fancy grocery store. I didn't buy them, obviously.

"Pine nuts," I say.

Cameron pops the container open and starts to eat. I walk over to him and he offers me some from his wet palm.

He smells good, like soap and damp skin. I breathe in deeply and then try to play it off like I'm sighing.

"What," he says.

"Nothing."

I take some pine nuts out of his hand and eat them. They're still moist from his skin.

"You never eat enough," he says.

"You would have no way of knowing that," I say in a way that I hope comes across as coy.

"Just...I remember it about you, I mean."

I take more pine nuts and inhale again because I'm standing so close to Cameron that I can smell wet hair and the soap Lucas has that I like the smell of and which Cameron must have used.

"Whatever," I say, and then I lean back a little and laugh. I forgot about Cameron because I haven't seen him in a while, but he's one of the few people I get along with easily. Or maybe I'm just drunk and this is a drunken thought, not that being drunk would necessarily make it untrue. "I like this song."

"Yeah," he says. "It's a good one." He pops the plastic top back on the pine nuts and then says, "you didn't want any more, did you?" and I shake my head and throw myself down on one of the weird modern chairs with a curved back. It's strangely easy to lounge in it dramatically despite its bizarre shape and Cameron looks down at me and smiles. I remember he once told me that he liked feeling like he was above me and I smile because I think I'm getting the sense that he's finding me attractive, and maybe it's because my date tonight so obviously wasn't, but I feel the stabs of desire in my stomach and think about what it would be like to pull Cameron down on top of me in this strange chair.

"I'm gonna go change," he says, and I stare at him and

nod. I give him my slow smile that means have sex with me and I think he gets it but he still walks away.

Thoughts idly drift across the surface of the shallow puddle that is my mind and one of them is: you're drunk and you should go to bed, but I want so badly to ignore reason and have a kiss.

"I'm gonna shower," I shout, and Cameron yells back what I think is "okay," and I figure the shower will be sobering enough that I either will or won't decide to have sex with him.

As soon as I stand naked in front of the mirror I start to examine every flaw in my face and body. I have a pimple on my forehead and cellulite in my stomach and thighs. I wish I could take a knife and razor off the parts of me that are ugly, but if I got started I think I would slowly peel away every inch of my skin until I was completely wet and raw.

I make the shower so hot that it stings and my eyes burn. I'm the kind of drunk that's starting to tip into nauseous and even though I feel sexy and beautiful I think it's probably wise to stay away from Cameron until morning. I'm glad that the bassist, at least, is probably someone I'll never see again.

When I get out of the shower I feel even uglier, like one of those little designer dogs that looks like a ferret after it gets groomed. I try not to look at myself in the mirror. I crawl back to the guest bedroom quietly, and I fall into a horrible drunken sleep without brushing my teeth or drinking any water.

* * *

I wake up with a headache and a mouth that tastes like the smell of a dead rat and I immediately remember that Cameron is here now, staying in the master bedroom. I wonder why I didn't move in there, and I guess it's because I just assumed that it would be an imposition, even though the imposition is that I'm here generally. Cameron's not afraid of imposing, it would seem, but boys never are.

I decide to go out into the back garden and look at what needs to be done, gardening-wise. Lucas said I don't have to garden but that I can if it makes me feel better about staying in the house, which it does. Even though I don't really feel like doing it.

I'm not careful to be quiet because I know Cameron is a heavy sleeper. Also he doesn't wake up before noon if he doesn't have to. He didn't when I knew him, at least.

The garden is pretty and I can tell it cost a lot of money to landscape it, but now it's tangled and choked with weeds. I don't know a lot about gardening but I know you're supposed to weed, so I guess that's what I'll do. I could use gloves, since there are a lot of roses, but I have a high pain tolerance and I don't want to waste time looking for gloves. Almost right away I start sweating so much that it hurts my eyes and I can barely see.

For some reason the physical discomfort feels good. I like the twinge in my back and the tight feeling in my hands when the thorns run through them. It's hot today but I wish it were hotter. I think about getting my phone and listening to music or getting a glass of water but something about the repetitive motion of weeding has lulled me into a trance and I feel like if I stop I might die.

After a while I hear Cameron in the kitchen making coffee with the fancy machine. I wonder how he knows how to make real coffee. Lucas does. I think about going inside and offering Cameron tea or breakfast or something, but I'm not the maid and I'm still masochistically enjoying the physical discomfort in my muscles from all the weeding. My back is crusted with sweat even though I'm just in a bathing suit now—I took my shirt off a while ago but left my pants on so my legs wouldn't get scratched up from the thorns.

"Hey," Cameron yells eventually. I half-expect him to offer me a cigarette or something, just from the tone of his voice and the way he's watching me, but he just says, "what are you doing?" and sits cross-legged in one of the Adirondack chairs with Lucas' yellow Le Creuset mug dangling from his hand.

"Gardening," I say.

Cameron's quiet for a while, ostensibly drinking his coffee, and I continue to weed. I've probably been at it for a few hours now and I've barely covered three square yards.

"Would you listen to music?" he asks. "I'm gonna get my speaker." He doesn't wait for me to answer, but I would have said yes anyway. Maybe he knows I would have wanted to, or maybe he just doesn't give a shit about what I want. Either way it's nice when he starts to play music. It's soft and slow music, and it makes me sad even though it's a sunny morning and I was feeling pretty good before.

He walks over to me so quietly that I don't hear him and then he murmurs, "holy shit."

I look up. "What?" I shield my face from the sun with my hand, and that's when I see that my hands are streaky with scratches and blood. I guess it was stupid not to wear gloves. "Are you okay?" he asks, reaching down and grabbing one of my hands with both of his.

"Yeah," I laugh. "I didn't notice." There's a dollop of blood slowly dripping down toward my eye—it landed on my forehead when I moved my hand to shield my face from the sun.

"Let me, um, let me see what Lucas has." He takes his hands away from me, and when he moves back toward the house I realize how cool it was standing in his shade; he's so tall that he blocked the sun.

I stand and watch him rifle around in Lucas' junk drawers, his gangly frame bumping into the corners of countertops and his long-fingered hands wrapping around what looks like a box of Band-Aids. From this distance and through the glass doors he's so perfect that he almost looks fake. I can tell his brow is furrowed and maybe it's because he's concerned about me but I can't think about anything except how much I want him—I want to touch his hair with my bloody hands and I want to find out what the skin on his neck smells like. I don't remember it even though I'm sure I must have known at one point.

When he comes back outside he crushes one of the rosebushes and I almost say something but then don't. He takes my hand again, the one that's more cut up, and dabs it with an alcohol wipe. "Does it burn?" he asks, and I shake my head no, even though it burns a little. "Jesus," he murmurs.

I look at my hand for a while, until it stops feeling like my hand and starts to feel like a disembodied limb floating in space. "It's really fucked up," Cameron says.

"It looks worse than it is," I say. I wonder why Cameron goes by Cameron and not Cam. He's one of those people whose names I never really say out loud, probably because his name is such a mouthful. But I always hear other people refer to him as Cameron. "How come no one calls you Cam?" I ask.

"What?" He turns his face down and the twist of his head unblocks the sun and blinds me for a moment. The heat across my forehead burns, and then so does my hand, and I squeeze Cameron's arm. I didn't realize that my other hand was wrapped around his upper arm, but it was. Just as my eyes start to adjust I realize that Cameron's staring at me, and then he moves his head again and I can see because there's no more sun and now he's kissing me. He pulls away and says, "sorry," and I ask, "why do you say that?" and he just stands there frowning, backlit by the sun.

I start to walk inside and he doesn't follow me so I turn around and raise my eyebrows and beckon him with my hand, the one that's less messed up. The other one is still tingling.

I open Lucas' sliding glass doors—I think these are French doors, though I've never been quite sure what French doors are, really—and I wait for Cameron to slip in quietly behind me. I lean against the glass and look at him. He's deliberately avoiding my gaze and I breathe in like I'm about to say something but really I just want him to look at me. I say nothing and start to chew on my lower lip in a way that I know he'll find attractive. He walks over to me and then our faces are almost touching and our lips brush against each other and he asks, "is this what you want, then?" and it's a dumb thing to say, so much so that I almost have to hold back a laugh, but I just nod. Then he really kisses me and I can feel every part of my body where it's pressing into the glass.

It's funny because in my memories of us sleeping together it didn't feel nearly this good, but maybe that's because it was a long time ago and we're both a little bit older now and we know how to do things.

He moves like he's going to take off my bathing suit top and then he pauses and pulls away. We're staring at each other and both breathing hard and he takes a breath like he's going to say something but he doesn't. He just kisses me again and I reach up to peel his shirt off. When I touch his skin it feels warm from the sun even though he was mostly standing in the shade. "Let's go..." I say, and I think about saying 'to my room,' but it's really Lucas' room. Cameron just nods and then pulls me into the hallway and then we're in the master bedroom. The floor is dotted with dark puddles that must be Cameron's discarded clothes—the curtains are drawn and it's dark, so dark that I can barely make anything out except for Cameron's hazy outline and the soft black hole of the bed.

He pushes me down onto the pillows. "Are you alright?" he asks, and I just nod into his shoulder because he's already climbing on top of me. I take off my bathing suit top and we press into each other and it feels so good to be touching someone that it makes me stop thinking.

"Do you want me to get a condom?" he asks eventually, and I say, "yes," and then he gets up and starts picking up pants from the ground.

"I don't know where my wallet is."

I'm naked on the bed and panting and I start to feel a bit like an animal. Cameron swears under his breath and throws another pair of shorts onto the ground. They make a clicking noise when they hit the wood floor, probably from the metal in his belt, and the noise makes me think again and I start to wonder if maybe we shouldn't be doing this, but I guess by now it's too late, and changing my mind would be bad manners. And I do, of course, want to have sex; it's just the fact that it's here and now and with Cameron that's making me rethink things.

"Got it," he says, and I hear the crinkling of plastic or foil or whatever it is that a condom wrapper is made of, and then he's coming over here and he's inside of me and I can't believe he stayed hard the whole time he was looking for the condom in his wallet.

I arch my back and wrap my legs around him because I know sometimes people like that—the only thing I remember about Cameron specifically is that he liked it when I kissed his neck, but I feel too shy to do that now— and he says, "fuck," and then after a little while longer, "you feel so good," and I don't say anything but my breath catches in my throat when I feel him whisper that into my ear.

After a while the ideal thing starts happening to me: I completely forget how to think and leave my mind for a few seconds but then Cameron ruins it by finishing. He kisses me smilingly on the side of my face and I laugh a little bit and then we're both laughing with what almost feels like relief and maybe it is relief, that we got this out of the way.

"That felt really good," I say and then instantly worry that I said the wrong thing. But he looks at me and then says, "yeah it did," and I can see in his black eyes that he really means it.

"What are you thinking about," he asks.

"Right now, or in general?" We both laugh.

"Right now," he says, and I look at him and lie.

"Nothing."

He looks at me for a while and eventually brushes a piece of hair away from my face which is so soft and sweet that it almost makes me shudder but I stop myself just in time. My eyes have adjusted to the dark now and I can see that I've left small smears of blood on the duvet and on Cameron's arms where I was holding them. The only light is leaking through the gaps in the curtains and underneath the door and it makes the blood look blue-black.

"Do you want to nap?" he asks, and I nod, even though I know there's no way I'll sleep.

"I don't know if we should get into the habit of sleeping in the same bed," I say, even though all I want to do is close my eyes and never wake up and have him be the last thing I feel.

"Will you not be comfortable here?" he asks, and it's such an innocent question that I want to lie back down and fall asleep backed into his body, where I know I'll feel safe. But I don't deserve that, so I pick up my bathing suit top from the ground and then stand up without putting it on. I'm just going across the hall, so there's not much of a need to get dressed.

"It's not that," I say.

"What," he asks, "Lucas?"

"No," I say, too quickly. "I just...I don't know." But I do know.

"Okay," he says, and then he lies down and closes his eyes, seemingly unbothered. I wonder if it makes a difference to him whether I stay or not. I could have just told him I wasn't tired enough to nap or that I needed to go write, but I guess this accomplishes the same thing in a worse way. I feel like I've done the wrong thing but I don't know whether it's because of the sex or because I've upset him by leaving.

"Do you want me to close the door?" I ask on my way out, shout-whispering so he knows I know he's trying to sleep.

"Leave it cracked, yeah," he says, and so I do, and all I see through the slit is the curve of his back. To me his body looks impossible but beautiful, like that painting—I can't remember the name of it—and I worry that I'm going to fall in love with him again.

Cameron

Out there with the roses, when I saw her, I don't know, it was so dramatic, and I thought maybe she had done something to hurt herself—not on purpose, but an accident, or something, and normally I think something like that would irritate me, you know, the drama, but when I saw her standing there with all those roses crushed on the ground around her, I just thought: I hope she's okay, I hope she's okay, I hope she's okay, and I was so relieved when she was, and I guess that's why it happened, not that it matters why it did, not that anyone's asking. It's not like she's Lucas' girlfriend. Lucas doesn't have a girlfriend, or maybe he does, but it's not her.

I wonder how long she'll stay.

Chapter Three

Desire is about lack and so is being a girl. I don't think this is a coincidence, but I guess it could be. I haven't seen Lucas since August and now September is basically over and it's starting to get cold.

Cameron's still here.

When I sit outside to look at the birds in the morning with my mug of tea, Cameron comes to join me. He's shirtless and I stare at his concave chest and long torso. We've had sex before, obviously, but I don't think I've ever had an unobstructed view of his body in such an exposed setting. He looks sinewy and birdlike. I told him he was sinewy once, I think, and he got angry at me.

"Hey." He folds himself into the chair next to mine and frowns at the bird feeders. He sits almost like a doll, with his limbs carefully bent and still. I'm jealous of how elegant it makes him look. "What are you doing?"

"Watching the birds."

"I thought you were afraid of birds."

"I can't believe you remember that."

It was over a week ago when we had sex and he's been

avoiding me since then. He went to the city and gave no reason for the trip and I'm almost sure he just went to get away from me. He came back with three boxes of soup dumplings from Pig Heaven and I ate almost two of them as my revenge. He hasn't said anything about it so I think he knows he did something wrong. That or he just didn't notice.

"Are you hungry?" he asks after a while, and I shrug. "I'm hungry," he says.

"I figured," I say.

"My friend Georgia is gonna come hang tonight." He takes out a pouch of tobacco and starts rolling a cigarette, and I can't tell whether he's doing it because he wants one or because he's nervous.

"Georgia?" I parrot like an idiot.

"Girl I went to college with." He says "went," like he dropped out, which maybe he did.

"What's she doing out here?" I ask, trying to seem completely unconcerned. She sounds beautiful and blonde and like I don't want to be confronted with her presence.

"We went to Australia together," he says, not answering my question. Rich people always have all this strange history with each other. I think anyone who's in their early twenties and has a complicated relationship with more than like two people is probably a terrifying sociopath. Which probably tracks for Cameron, actually.

"You can have dinner with us."

"Do you want me to?" I frown. "I can also go into town or something." Even as I say it I know I'm not considering it seriously. I'll eat dinner with them whether they want me to or not.

"No," he says. "I mean, no, don't go into town." And then, when I don't say anything, he turns to me with his big black eyes with their slick dark lashes and asks, "are you hungry?"

* * *

Before dinner I lock myself in Lucas' room and blast whiny, girly music that I know Cameron won't like. Eventually he knocks on my door and I think it's going to be to tell me to turn the music off, but he just wants me to come to the grocery store. I wonder if he's asking me that because he likes being around me or because he's just too much of a fucking idiot to know how to grocery shop for a dinner.

"What are we even eating?" I ask when we're in the car. We take Lucas' Mini Cooper convertible because Cameron wants to. Lucas told me I could drive it around but I haven't dared yet and I probably never will. I'd be too afraid of getting a scratch on it.

"I don't know," Cameron shouts over the music. "What do you want?"

I laugh.

"What?" he asks.

"Nothing," I say. "I don't know." I think about how he definitely just wanted me to come so that I would shop and then cook everything for dinner. And I probably will.

"Let's just make pasta," I say, "even though I remember you don't like it," at the same time that he says, "I don't like pasta," and then we both laugh self-consciously and he turns down the music.

He has sunglasses on even though it's dusk and not a very clear evening, and his eyes are trained on the road except I can occasionally detect him glancing at me through the gap between the glasses and his face. I left my sunglasses on the bedside table after I tried them on in front of the mirror and decided they make me look like a boy.

"So," I say, "why don't we just make pizza."

"What do you mean?" he asks, frowning. I remember why I used to like him so much—this frown, like a confused puppy when a door slams somewhere in the house and it doesn't know how to react.

"Like. Dough, cheese, tomato sauce. Basil. If we want to go crazy."

"Okay, okay," he says, and then laughs. "But how do we make them ourselves?"

"I'll show you," I say. "It's easy." Then I reach out and turn the music back up, because the song changed and now it's something I like, something I remember Cameron showing me a long time ago. I wonder if he remembers—I think he probably doesn't and now it's just a song he likes.

When we get to the grocery store he takes his sunglasses off and tosses them in the backseat. I think about saying he should be more careful or they'll get crushed, but I say nothing.

"Do we need a big cart, you think?" I ask when we're by the entrance. There's a heaping display of squashes and pumpkins and Cameron's turning a particularly warty green one over in his hands. It makes me think about how it felt when he touched me. He has big hands, bigger than Lucas', not that there's a natural comparison between the two of them other than their relation to me. "Um, or just a basket."

"I don't know," he says, placing the squash down carefully atop a pyramid of pumpkins. "What do you think?"

"Probably just a basket, then," I say, and then he walks through the sliding doors and says, "I want to get some stuff for the week, too," and I resist the urge to ask him how long he thinks he's going to be staying.

He seems to be walking purposefully, but then he lingers at the display of Tate's cookies at the end of the aisle. He runs his long fingers over the lip of a bag of white chocolate macadamia ones and then he frowns and seems to think better of it. "Do we have any peanut butter?" he asks. I nod and then realize that he can't see me. "Yeah," I say. "No jam or anything, though." He nods and veers toward the produce section and it occurs to me that I would be happy just following him around the grocery store, walking in circles forever. It smells clean in here and everything is so brightly colored and also it's the Hamptons so all the food is fancy and packaged nicely.

Cameron grabs a mango, then stops three more from falling. "You like these, right?" he asks, and I nod, and he's looking at me this time. He smiles and grabs three of them and then bumps into me with his upper body. I laugh and say, "let's get apples." We start to get giddy—or at least I do—and we walk up and down the aisles looking at the different food and talking about what we like and don't like. The basket looks heavy already and I'm glad Cameron's carrying it. It makes me think about how it's so much easier to shop and cook for two people rather than one person, which is something I always heard adults say growing up but didn't really understand until now.

"Annie's Mac," I say.

"Disgusting," he says.

"That's right," I say. "You don't like pasta." He looks at me and grins and then bumps me again. "We have to get canned tomatoes," I say, and I throw San Marzanos in the basket because who cares, if I'm going to be at a weird uncomfortable dinner I may as well enjoy the food. "Shouldn't we use fresh," he says, and I stick my tongue out. "No way," I say, "and I'm in charge." He snorts and bumps me again and then we're both giggling and I wonder if the old people and Pilates housewives milling around think we're a cute couple. They're probably not paying attention to us at all. "Fresh mozz," I say once the giggles subside.

"Freshhhh moooozzzz," he says, drawing out the words in a fake-deep voice to make fun of me.

On our walk to the cheese section he picks up some chocolate chip muffins. "Would you eat these?" he asks.

"If you want them," I say.

"You're in charge," he says.

He throws them in the basket. In the produce section the sprinklers turn on and spray cold misty water on the vegetables. I shiver even though it's hot outside. It's always cold in the grocery store, I guess, but that's not why I'm shivering. I think it's because I'm happy. "Are you hungry?" Cameron asks, and I nod. "It's bad to go grocery shopping when you're hungry," I say, but he just rubs an apple on his shirt and then hands it to me, already taking a bite out of another one, and I know that when we leave we won't pay for them.

* * *

I hear Georgia get in and I decide to pout in Lucas' room for a bit longer and pretend that I was 'working' when I come out. Cameron probably wants time alone with her, anyway.

They're laughing and there's lots of clattering and then their voices fade. It sounds like Cameron's bringing her to the back room. I hear them giggling again pretty quickly which means that they didn't fuck, or at least not right away when he showed her the room. I shut my laptop very gently and slowly and then lie on my back on the bed with a book open next to me so that I can always say I was reading, just in case. But napping is also a reasonable excuse.

Glasses clink and I guess they must be drinking. I wonder why they don't go outside. It's decent weather and soon it'll be winter and freezing and completely unbearable.

While I'm ruminating about this Cameron calls my name and then I hear him walk a little closer and call it again.

"I'll come out," I shout, and then I wonder whether I should change out of my sweatpants and bikini top. Maybe it's a power move to come out wearing that, though.

When I walk into the living room I'm immediately depressed. Georgia is, of course, blonde and beautiful and perfect. She's wearing a little bit of makeup, probably, but I can tell that under the makeup her skin is glowing and pore-less. I feel hatred and contempt for her but then she's smiling at me and saying, "Cam told me about you," so I have to grin back and say, "don't believe everything you hear," and she gives a tinkling little fairy laugh. She has pink acrylic nails that brush against my back when she puts down her wineglass to hug me hello. She smells like vanilla perfume and something else, like fruit that's about to rot. But it's not entirely a bad smell and I think if she weren't Cameron's ambiguous-how-close-are-they friend I might even be attracted to her. Also she's wearing a mesh miniskirt which makes me feel like a dumpy freak in my sweats.

"We're going to make pizza," Cameron says lamely.

Georgia turns to him and says, "you said that already."

Cameron shrugs moodily and I wonder if it's my presence that's pissing him off now or if Georgia's been annoying him the whole time. She seems annoying enough but also she's pretty and boys never tend to be the ones who realize when a pretty girl is being annoying.

For a while we loiter around and drink and chat about nothing. I don't drink yet because I want to maintain the upper hand. I'm being cold, I can tell, but it's not like anyone else is making a grand effort either. I always hate when things like this happen and I'm forced to hang out with people I don't get along with. It reminds me that the world is full of those kinds of people.

"I wish it was still summer," Georgia says, and no one says anything. Of course she wishes it were still summer. Everyone does. She's glaring at Cameron who nonchalantly drinks his fancy beer, his bare feet resting on the deck like it's a velvet pillow. "How long have you and Lucas been together?" Georgia asks me with a seemingly innocent curiosity.

"Oh," I say, "we're not together." Cameron swallows and then clinks his glass down against his plate. "We're just best friends."

"That's so funny," she says. "*Cameron* was telling me the other day...that *he* was best friends with you."

"Lucas?"

"No, *Cameron*."

"Oh," I say, making every effort not to look at Cameron or smile. "That is funny." No one laughs. "I have lots of best friends."

"I do too, I guess," she says, and then she starts scrolling on her phone. "God, I don't want to go back to school." Georgia sighs theatrically and the ends of her blonde hair bounce.

"Don't, then," Cameron says, smiling. He's either drunk now or just in a better mood. One of his legs is folded underneath him, and he looks too big and skinny for the chair he's in. It makes me want to offer him a different chair which makes me feel like my mother. I guess we all become our mother eventually no matter how much we hate her. Not that there's anything specific wrong with my mom, she's just a cunt.

"Do you want a vodka tonic?" Georgia asks. "I'm going to make a vodka tonic."

"No thanks."

"Have one," Cameron says. "Don't be lame."

I smile and say, "fine, I'll have one if you do," and he glowers at me.

"I already have a beer," he says.

"Don't be lame," I say, in the same mock voice he used on me earlier in the grocery store, except then we were having fun and now we're not. Georgia takes vodka from the shelf and I laugh out loud so she knows it's all a game.

"Do you have a job?" Georgia asks, pouring what looks like three shots of vodka into each glass. "Because you graduated, right?"

"I did graduate," I say. "But I have no job."

"Oh," she says.

"She's writing a novel," Cameron says, then "don't be modest." He kicks me under the table and I know what he really means to say is, 'stop being such a fucking bitch,' but it's too late; I've already started and I can't switch gears now.

"Wow," says Georgia, in the tone of someone who is not impressed at all. "That's so cool."

"It's not, really," I say. "It's the only thing I've ever known how to do."

"I'm sure you know how to do lots of other stuff," Georgia says, and Cameron snorts.

"I can cook," I say, grinning with the specific pleasure of making some little blonde bitch uncomfortable. Georgia is exactly the type of girl who would have tortured people like me and Cameron in high school merely by existing and being so effortless and perfect. Her pink acrylics tap clickingly on the table after she sets down everyone's drinks. She spills Cameron's a little bit and a seeping puddle of liquid turns the white marble a darker, cloudier white. If I were more worried about these kinds of things or if the table were a different material I would have cleaned up the spill right away, but instead I just watch as it creeps toward the edge and then eventually starts dripping onto the floor, narrowly missing Cameron's leg. He's wearing Carhartt pants and he looks better than he's ever looked and I wonder if it's just because Georgia's here and receiving some of his attention, but I want him very badly again.

"Why aren't *you* in school?" I ask, experimenting to see how much of a cunt I can be. She doesn't catch that I'm being mean and she just sighs and then smiles at Cameron.

"School's boring," she says. I feel almost bad for her because she's so pretty that when she stops being that way I'm sure it will be very jarring for her.

"Boring how?" I ask, resisting the urge to ask her what she studies. I know it's a dull question but I want the jolt of satisfaction in my superiority when she says marketing or communications or nursing.

"Boring because I've been there for three years now... and I'm over it."

"Do you need another drink?" Cameron asks, at the same time that I push back from the table and say, "let's go outside."

Georgia smiles and seems to be happy at the prospect of getting nearer to the pool probably because she wants to go swimming and show off her body which is undoubtedly perfect in every major way.

"Here." Cameron goes to the fridge and pulls out a beer, another one of his special beers that he made a big show of getting earlier at the grocery store. He gives one to me and then asks, "what do you want, Georgie?" and even though he's calling her by a cute little nickname I have the wet slimy beer can in my hand, which proves that I'm the one who gets him and that it's me and him who are allied here, if not in real love.

"Is there tequila?" Georgia yells through the gaping French doors which are already flung open, letting the night air and the dusky mosquitoes spill across the threshold.

"No," I say, even though I'm not totally sure. There could be tequila around here somewhere but also if she wanted tequila she should have fucking brought some. I don't like when people are entitled to other people's things but I guess that's really rich coming from me, in Lucas' house. But at least I fuck him. Georgia seems like she wouldn't.

Cameron perches on the edge of one of the weird patio chairs and I can tell he's uncomfortable because he doesn't fold his body into the chair the way he normally would. Also one of his bony fingers is tapping against the side of his beer can. He has massive fingers and it takes me a long time to tear my eyes away from them.

"What," I say. He's been staring at me, too. So it was a mutual watching.

"Nothing," he says. "Are you tired?" I just nod and at this point Georgia comes outside with a full wineglass and I can't ask him if he's tired too.

Georgia didn't ask to be so blonde and bubbly. But then again she's probably not a natural blonde and no one's exactly naturally bubbly. She did switch from wine to hard liquor and back again, though, which usually indicates some form of extreme suffering.

We all sit for a while and Cameron and Georgia start to reminisce about Australia and random things and people they have in common. I start to glaze over a bit and I wonder whether I should leave, but then Cameron says, "sorry, I know this is annoying," and I say, "yes, it is."

Georgia frowns. "Do you ever do anything?" she asks. Her wineglass is empty.

"Me?"

"Georgia," Cameron says.

"*What*," she says, and her legs which were crossed so primly before are now skewed at a strange angle and I can see razor burn where the edge of her bikini bottom digs into her skin. "Does she just sit around here?"

I laugh very cruelly and raise my beer can in Georgia's direction, but I look at Cameron instead of her. "No," I say. "She's right." This makes everyone quiet for a little while and I can tell Cameron's thinking about how to make this all not be happening.

"Um," Cameron says, "what are you doing tomorrow?"

"Why are you asking *her*," Georgia says, and that's when I stand up.

"Don't," Cameron says, and I don't know whether the don't is for Georgia or for me standing up. Either way I win.

"Let's...maybe I'll go get a...board game," I say, but Cameron is looking helplessly at Georgia and then he shakes his head at me. I sit back down. I'll give it five minutes and then I'm leaving him to handle it.

"I kind of hate it here," Georgia says. "It's not fun."

Cameron looks at her and then at me and I can tell he's not even remotely equipped to deal with what's happening.

"The Hamptons?" I ask, "or Lucas' house specifically?"

"I don't even know who Lucas *is*," she says, and I can tell she's about to cry. I have to leave. I didn't want this and anyway we didn't end up making pizzas, we just got drunk and I think everyone's probably fucking starving. I am. But also I'm a little nauseous. I stand up and feel for a second like the sky with its endless spray of stars could just as easily be the ground if I squinted a certain way.

"I'm going to go to sleep," I say. "But...I'll see you in the morning, Gina."

"Georgia."

"Sorry," I say, even though I'm not. "Sleep well, guys." I stand up and leave my half-empty drink on the table. I know I'll probably end up cleaning tomorrow, but it's nice to think that I might be leaving it for Cameron to deal with.

As soon as the door to my room clicks shut I can hear her raising her voice at him. In a way I respect girls like that, girls who don't take shit and yell at rude, emotionally unavailable men. But I've always been more in it for the long game. I'd let a man manipulate me for seventeen years if I thought it meant even a half-second of true, tortured romance.

I've decided that they haven't slept together but that they've maybe hooked up, and this weekend she was trying to fuck him. I construct an elaborate version of their history —played across the IMAX screen of my mind—where they see each other at parties but one of them is always a little too fucked-up or a little too involved with someone else. Georgia's bored with liberal arts college and single and looking for adventure and Cameron's an edgy (and I mean this relatively, of course) stoner with terrible prospects. But men with terrible prospects who don't have their shit together always seem to stumble across good things. Kismet or serendipity or whatever you want to call it.

Anyway I think Georgia was looking for a sexy, grungy time that she could go brag to her sorority sisters about to seem like the interesting one. Every little blonde girl just wants a taste of that bad boy edge. But fortunately or unfortunately (depending on how you look at it), Georgia isn't willing to debase and humiliate herself enough to run with the wolves. The wolves, in this case, being me and Cameron. I crack a smile looking at the wall. If I were uglier none of these people would have anything to do with me.

The shouting subsides and I wonder if they went to bed or if maybe they're fucking. I doubt they'd be hooking up but they are drunk and of course that's where my brain goes. I don't have any claim to Cameron, anyway, and I know that if I decided that I did then I still wouldn't and that's the terrible part. I lie down in bed flat on my back just like I was when Georgia got here. It's dark outside and the house is sinister like it always is at night, with artificial light leaking through the endless windows, and the fluttering curtains, and the ever-present feeling of being observed. There's not much of a moon tonight so it's all orange-creamsicle-glow and blue-dark casting shadows that look ominous, probably because they're all cast by Lucas' weird, expensive furniture.

I think about how I should probably take a shower but I don't really feel like it and then there's a knock on my door.

"Hey," and before I heard the familiar vibrating edge of the voice, I thought it was going to be the distraught Georgia looking for female comfort (which she would not have found). But of course it's Cameron. I open the door and he hovers on the threshold for a second. Do bedrooms even have thresholds, I don't know, my brain has stopped working a little bit because I can smell Cameron and also the hoppy smell of the weird craft beer he was drinking all night. "Do you want to come and smoke?"

I nod and then turn around to get a sweater and Cameron follows me. We're completely silent and it feels very high school, like he's not supposed to be in my room or wake up my parents. I can tell that he's drunk and I'm not really very drunk, I just had the one vodka drink and half a beer, and I know he probably wants me or at least wants *something* from me and when men want *something* it's usually sex. But *sometimes* it's more complicated than that.

I pull a sweater out of the drawer where I keep them and I think for a second about taking off my bikini top before pulling it on but Cameron already knows what my body looks like and I'm worried it'll come off as desperate. I pull the sweater on and then decide that I'll change my pants from sweatpants to a different pair of sweatpants, in the spirit of seduction.

"Sorry," I whisper. "I'm really cold." I'm not wearing underwear which makes me feel a little self-conscious about changing my pants but Cameron doesn't even look or if he does he hides it well.

"It's okay," he says, and I want to walk over to him and put my whole head inside his mouth. He's already rolling us cigs and I kind of thought when he said want to smoke he meant weed, and I can't tell whether this bodes better or worse for the state of our relationship.

We walk outside and I make sure to guide the door to the bedroom shut so that it doesn't slam. It makes a gentle half-click and then I follow Cameron. He's standing in the partly open doorway to the backyard, his outline framed by the pool light and his whole body glowing, like he's not even real and if he were real he'd be a sad angel who could never belong to me.

We sit on the ledge of the back porch even though the patio furniture is scattered everywhere. Cameron lights his cigarette first and then hands me mine and the lighter, almost as an afterthought. I wonder if he invited me out here because I'm me or because he just didn't want to be alone. Either way it's me and not Georgia.

It sounds like crickets and quiet and it is cold even though there's still the memory of summer in the air and I let Cameron melt into the quiet for a while. I can hear his slow breathing and I wonder if he can hear mine or if he's so off in his own head that I'm not real to him. Our elbows and knees are intermittently brushing and every time the fabric of our clothes rubs past each other I feel like someone is wrapping their arms around my entire body and squeezing it.

"What happened?" I finally ask.

"She tried to have sex with me," he says, grinning sheepishly. I wonder why he doesn't lie to me.

"Well." I blow a plume of smoke out of the side of my

mouth, the side that Cameron isn't on. "You did invite her here."

"She invited herself, really," he says, and I guess it's a testament to my knowledge of how passive I know boys like him can be that I kind of believe him. She seems like a take-charge kind of gal and he, I know, is someone who just lets things happen to him. Like a woman.

"Still," I say. "You let her come." I worry I'm overdoing it with this because he's quiet while he takes a drag and then ashes onto the deck. His hand is shaking a little bit. His hands never shake, not that I've seen.

"What *is* going on?" he asks quietly. "With you and Lucas."

"Nothing," I say right away. "I haven't seen him since August."

"August," he says, like he's trying out how the word feels in his mouth. "That's...a while ago."

"Yeah," I say, and then we sit and smoke and say nothing. When I finish my cigarette he puts his out and says, "we can go inside if you want," and I say, "do you want to," and he says, "not really."

"If it were warmer we could swim," I say, knowing full well that we'd never do anything like that together, especially not with Georgia here.

"Nah," he says, and then we smoke in silence. My leg leans into his and I don't move it away. His skin gives just a little bit even though it's hard and solid. It's like one of those Greek statues where hard stone fingers dig into the woman's thigh and make it look pillow-soft even though it's thick and solid and made of marble.

"What are you thinking," he asks. I could tell him that I'm thinking about Greek statues but then I remember that boys think it's sexy when you're quiet and mysterious. If I reveal my thoughts then I stop being compelling and start becoming irritating. I just shake my head and blow smoke from the side of my mouth. Cameron is letting his cigarette burn between his fingers and the tiny puffs of steam coming from his nose are only there because of how warm his breath is. "What?" He laughs and I shake my head again. He puts his hand behind me and props himself up. I lean back involuntarily into the curve of his arm and when we're touching like that I feel completely calm even with Georgia and the nicotine and the general discomfort of Lucas' house. On my hand—the one holding the cigarette—there are faint white lines from when weeding got me all scratched up. Cameron sees me looking at it and runs his thumb over the line of one of the scars.

"Why?" I ask, and then I remember that with boys it's never a good idea to start a question with why. "What...are *you* thinking?" He doesn't say anything and we just sit and I know we're probably both thinking the same thing but also other people's thoughts are an unsolvable mystery and it's possible we're thinking the opposite thing (or worse, that our thoughts aren't connected at all). I feel so melodramatic and I don't know if Cameron makes me feel this way or if it's the idea of Cameron, the boy that I used to know in high school who is different and sad now. And of course I'm different too, and yet we still find each other attractive, and isn't there something *beautiful*, something *profound* about that.

"I'm tired," he says, and he really sounds it. He sounds older than me. "Do you want to go to bed." He says it like a statement, not a question. Like it's already been decided what I want, even though I can't even tell whether he's asking me if I want to go to bed or if I want to go to bed with him. I know I have to answer carefully.

"Not yet," I say. My cigarette is almost gone but I take another drag. I feel the heat on my fingers and I wish I could communicate to Cameron how badly I want him, how much better I feel when he's touching me.

He shifts a little bit and I lean away from him and he breathes in like he's about to say something so I look at him and bite my lip. He doesn't say anything. I think about kissing him and I know he can probably tell that I'm thinking about it but he doesn't do anything and I can't tell whether he wants me. I can smell him and I can't think. He smells purely sweet, like a baby, like cinnamon, even though he's been drinking beer and smoking all night.

"Will you," I say, and then I stop talking and push my hair away from my face.

"What," he says, and then I do kiss him, and I feel like an idiot because he kisses me back only slightly and then inhales sharply and says, "sorry," and I say, "sorry, sorry," and then we look at each other and then he says, "I want to," and I know it's not true because our faces are inches apart and if he wanted to he would.

"I should go," I say, and then I stand up. "to...um...to bed."

"Yeah." He clears his throat. "I'm sorry."

"For what?" I wish I could say what I wanted to say but somehow it's impossible here, by the pool. It smells like jasmine again even though I don't see any jasmine in Lucas' entire fucking backyard. There are some pink flowers climbing their way up the trellis that leans against the wall but they're not jasmine. I don't know a lot about anything but I do know that. A firefly blinks in the middle distance and for a second I almost feel like praying, but I can't take myself seriously enough and I don't want Cameron to think I'm waiting for him to say something to me.

"Good night," I say, and as I walk through the giant French doors I hear him inhale like he's going to say something but then he says nothing, nothing at all.

Cameron

I fucked Georgia, of course I fucked Georgia, but it didn't mean anything—I mean not that it ever does, but with Georgia it especially didn't. I don't think I could tell you a single thing we ever spoke about, not that I could really tell you anything about anyone, but with her (with her, not Georgia—it was a long time ago) I remember climbing up the side of a building, somewhere we weren't supposed to be, but it was icy, and she slid, and she kicked me in the face, and my nose was bleeding, and she thought it was so funny, and she licked the blood from under my nose, and we talked about what it would be like when we were older—not between us, but in general, in our lives, and I remember that. I don't know why. For no reason, I guess. It's just a memory.

Chapter Four

In the morning I think about hiding out in my room but then I realize that I have more of a right to be here than anyone (arguably) and that I shouldn't let the specter of Georgia ruin my morning. I want to make tea, anyway. And there are those muffins that Cameron and I bought at the grocery store.

I get up and wash my face and put on a dress, like a regular girl. The dress is long and white and pretty, but it makes me look pale and like I'm trying too hard, so I take it off and put on baggy jeans and a t-shirt that says: Anxiety has Many Faces But There is Only One Xanax. I stole it from someone I used to sleep with.

When I get to the kitchen Cameron and Georgia are sitting at the table in complete silence. There's a white crust underneath Georgia's acrylics that could be food or come or toothpaste. I stare at it while everyone drinks silently and I think about making a joke or something but then I remember that not everyone's a morning person, especially not Cameron. Also it probably isn't come under her nails because she didn't have sex with anyone last night so it's definitely food which is less fun and more embarrassing. I wonder if she ate last night after I went to bed which makes me wonder if she heard me and Cameron talking outside. She probably did. Girls like her seem like they miss everything but they don't miss stuff like that.

"Morning, guys," I say, and neither of them says anything back.

Cameron's drinking instant coffee which feels appropriate for him but when he offers some to Georgia she wrinkles her nose and says, "no," and then vaguely mentions going to Starbucks, but more like she wants someone else to go and less like she wants to go herself. Obviously Cameron won't go and in lieu of offering to go I say, "you could have some tea," and gesture to the electric kettle.

She chooses a rose tea but I don't think she knows it's the herbal kind. She puts it the PROUD REPUBLICAN mug that Lucas drinks from ironically—but will probably grow into— and I wonder if she's an actual Republican. She's blonde enough. While I'm watching them both drink in strained silence I actually start to enjoy myself. I wonder vaguely if this makes me a bad person.

"Shit weather," I say, and no one says anything. It's overcast which makes everyone's skin look very luminous in comparison. "But I bet it'll burn off by the afternoon. It usually does." Still no one speaks, and now I'm grinning. "We're so close to the water...you know."

Georgia glowers at me and then starts talking about how she doesn't want to miss her train and I ask, "oh, you're leaving already?" and Cameron explains on her behalf that she's going to see some people in the city and that her friend the club promoter is going to get her and her friends into some shitty club where Kendall Jenner will most probably also be.

"Wow," I say. "That sounds really fun." Cameron glances at me and I know he can tell I'm being sarcastic. I look at Georgia and I think about how I kind of won in the game against her, at least in this specific instance. She's going to a club in the city where she will potentially see a lot of models and I'm staying here where I'll be the most beautiful (and only) girl. Georgia had maybe one sip of her tea and when she gets up I realize that she must be already packed because she and Cameron walk right to the door. She does not say goodbye to me, but I smile and wave at her slim back and then flip her off which makes me feel like a little bit of a baby, but a baby who won.

They walk out the door and I listen to Cameron say something and then hear the slam of the trunk. Georgia doesn't say anything, or if she does I don't hear her. Neither of them is laughing, and if I didn't know them I might think they were a couple that's been together for a long time, or two people who don't know each other very well.

* * *

While Cameron's at the train station I can't write or focus on anything because all I can think about is how he didn't fuck me last night and even though he didn't fuck Georgia either it still feels like a brutal rejection and I feel ugly in my body mind and soul. I wish it were possible to reach into someone's head and pull out their brain and unravel their thoughts like film strips to run through a projector and play back on the wall.

I can never tell what anyone's thinking, especially once they've had sex with me. The more recently I've had sex with someone, the more impossible it is for me to know what they're thinking. Before I have sex with someone I know exactly what they're thinking, most of the time, and it's: I wonder if me and that girl are ever gonna fuck.

I start to eat a pear. I think about Lucas. I wonder if the relationship that Lucas has with me is closer to the one that Cameron has with Georgia than it is to the one that Cameron has with me. I realize that I don't really want Lucas to come back. At least not like I did before.

When the pear is half-gone and my eyes are crossed and unfocused I have a useful thought, for once, and I finally start to write. It makes me stop thinking in the same way that sex does, even though writing obviously requires at least some degree of thinking.

An hour or so later Cameron comes back and for once he's actually interrupting my writing. The kitchen is flooded with crisp early fall light and the square of sky that's visible through the skylight is a clear and painful blue.

"What are you doing?" he asks.

"Working," I say, even though it's not work because I don't get paid for it. I should just say I'm doing nothing.

"Don't you usually work in your room?" He opens the fridge and then closes it without taking anything from it.

I nod. "Nice light out here today," I say, and then I click the screen of my laptop shut.

He walks over so that he's standing across from me, propping his body on the counter. I stand up from my chair and lean against the island.

"I'm sorry it was weird last night," he says, and I say, "you're not obliged to apologize to me," and then we just stare at each other and he fiddles with his watch which I never really noticed he wore until now. Maybe he only just started wearing it.

"Is your watch new?" I ask, and I reach my hand out to touch it but I think he thinks I'm reaching my hand out for something else because he pushes off the counter and presses me against the island and kisses me. I take a breath after a few seconds to say something but then I can't remember what it was I wanted to say.

I hear the bell-like clinking that means he's undoing his belt and it gives me déjà vu not because it's him but because it's a sound that I heard in this exact place a few years ago when I was here with Lucas and we fucked on this same kitchen island. I am briefly unsure who it is that's touching me, but then I open my eyes.

It hasn't even been two minutes since he walked in the door and he's already ripping my jeans off and they get caught around one of my ankles and he says, "shit," and then he's inside of me and I can't believe how quickly it's happening and how he didn't use a condom or anything, but it feels good and inevitable like it's always already happened like this.

I crane my neck back and it feels like if I'm not careful my head could snap off. For a moment I open my eyes and they're flooded with the awful, beautiful blue of the sky, and I wish for that moment that I could be the type of person who is content in the world. Then I shut my eyes again and Cameron's shuddering breath in my ear gets louder.

When he finishes he stares at me for a long time and then says, "fuck," and I just nod. Even though I know everyone experiences things differently I feel like we might have just felt the same.

Cameron slumps onto me, his head on my chest, and I let my eyes get unfocused while I look at the spot on the handle of one of the kitchen cabinets that reflects the golden light of the afternoon sun. "I'm sorry," he mumbles into my shoulder, and I ask, "why?" even though I know what he's about to say. "We can't keep doing this," he whispers, and I think about saying why not, but why is the worst question you can ask a man you're sexually involved with because sex makes them behave irrationally and if you remind them of that then they might remember that they don't really like you.

Ironically as he says this, he's still literally inside me and catching his breath and as he pulls out of me I wonder if maybe it isn't irony, if maybe it's something else.

Cameron

shouldn't have done that shouldn't have done that
shouldn't have done that shouldn't have done that
shouldn't have done that shouldn't have done that
shouldn't have done that shouldn't have done that
shouldn't have done that shouldn't have done that
shouldn't have done that shouldn't have done that
shouldn't have done that shouldn't have done that
shouldn't have done that shouldn't have done that
shouldn't have done that shouldn't have done that
shouldn't have done that shouldn't have done that
shouldn't have done that shouldn't have done that
shouldn't have done that shouldn't have done that
shouldn't have done that shouldn't have done that
shouldn't have done that shouldn't have done that
shouldn't have done that shouldn't have done that
shouldn't have done that shouldn't have done that
shouldn't have done that shouldn't have done that
shouldn't have done that shouldn't have done that
shouldn't have done that shouldn't have done that

Chapter Five

It goes without saying that I'm not working on my novel because all I can do is think about sex.

I lie in Lucas' bed which is sort of now my bed and think about sex with Lucas and then eventually I start to think about sex with other people. Sometimes I even think about sex with other people first. Cameron usually features somewhere in the order but thinking about that makes me feel bad about myself because he seemed to stop wanting me for no reason. The past few weeks he's been avoiding me and being quiet around the house which is somehow worse than if he weren't here at all.

I don't even masturbate while I'm thinking, not usually. I just stare at the ceiling and think about sex until I get painfully depressed. It's been so long since someone who actually cared about me touched me.

While I'm in bed this morning I can hear Cameron showering down the hall. I think that sometimes the interesting and exciting thing is not sleeping with someone, even though at the time I always think having sex is going to be the good choice. All this being said, I've made plans to go into the city later today to see some guy I know who I'll probably have sex with. Sex is how I know him in the first place, so there wouldn't be another reason he'd want to see me. In a way this type of arrangement is very calming to me.

Cameron is staying here and I think it'll be good for him to wait around alone in the palace of windows for a change. Probably he'll have a great time and I'm the only one who can't stand to be alone here.

When I hear Cameron get out of the shower I have chest pain. I wonder vaguely if I'm having a heart attack from all the smoking and lack of sleep. I kind of hope that I am.

I'm still alive when Cameron knocks on my door, after ten minutes of silence. He's standing there damp and radiant and asking me, "are you hungry?" and I tell him I don't have time to eat before I go. He looks wounded and I know it's over, it's all over; I would do anything for him. Before I can say I'll eat with him, I'll stay, I won't go to New York, he's turning around and saying, "have fun in the city," and it's hard not to believe that he doesn't love me.

* * *

By late afternoon I'm on the LIRR into the city to see the actor boy who I know from sex. He thinks I'm just going to happen to be in the city, not that I'm coming in to see him. I told him I'd be visiting friends. It's all a very fun and complicated game that I never quite feel like I'm winning. But this boy is very attractive, so attractive that even being around him makes me feel better about my own physical appearance.

I don't know if Cameron and I will ever have sex again and I've done a pretty good job of convincing myself that I don't care. I'll fuck this actor boy and everything will be just fine. I say this to myself over and over, like a prayer.

Outside the train window the sun is setting and the sky is cracked open leaking orange and pink like some kind of pale jewel, and I wish I were doing something other than going to see some stupid boy who doesn't even really like me. I stare out the window and wonder how it is that anything could be so achingly beautiful.

The sunset always happens quickly but somehow also over an infinitely broken apart spray of moments, so that I feel like I'm looking out the window and bending time. Really I'm just shifting my thighs around trying to get comfortable which is impossible to do because I'm bored and horny. I think about the last time I had sex with this guy. He fucked me from behind standing up and then said he had never done it like this before with anyone, which I thought was strange because it wasn't like I was hanging upside down from a harness or anything, I was just standing up gripping the back of the couch in his parents' basement. It made me wonder if maybe he doesn't have sex with a lot of people but I think it could also be that he's just one of those guys who usually only has sex with girls he respects and therefore doesn't always get to fuck them from behind.

I take out a book and try to read and an hour later we pull into Penn Station. It's not as pretty as Grand Central and it's so sad because it used to be really gorgeous. But so much of the world is like this. I think being in New York City is making me more romantic and wistful than I already am, which is probably not a good thing.

I walk around for most of the evening and it's good fall weather, not too hot but not exactly cool, and once I get hungry I sit at some cheap burrito place and read my book for a little while. It's nice to be somewhere that isn't quiet. The city is the only place where I ever really feel invisible and it's one of my favorite feelings. There're so many people, so many beautiful people, and no one bothers to look at me. I can watch everyone and do whatever I want and no one cares. Not that people care normally, but they do look, and it's not the looking that bothers me so much as the perception.

I'm supposed to meet Tom at a bar. That's his name. I try not to say or even think boys' names because they can sense that and then they think you're crazy. It's like how whenever you save a boy's number in your phone you're destined never to see him again. Better to know them by their area codes. But I'm literally on my way to see Tom, so I can think his name without fucking things up, I hope. The bar is a forty-five minute walk from where I am now but I know I'll make the walk much faster, so I kill time by buying a pack of cigarettes and then smoking one outside of the bodega. It was stupid to buy cigarettes here, they're insanely expensive, but it does waste about ten minutes because I bought light blue American Spirits and smoking one of those is an event. I finally start to walk to the bar and the walking combined with the delicate burn of the cigarette makes me feel mentally very clear and maybe also close to God.

* * *

There are too many people at the bar. It's so many people, in fact, that I resolve to be scowly and antisocial until Tom takes me home. I end up talking to two English girls, fashion students who hate London and that's why they're here. I don't understand how you could hate London and love New York, but I do listen to them talk about the Miu Miu show for about fifteen minutes without them noticing that I haven't said anything.

"Do you find Americans to be worse than English people?" I ask one of them because I assume she'll have a lot to say about it, and she tosses her buttery hair over one shoulder and asks, "what do you mean, worse?" and the other one says, "Americans are the only people in the world who can act spoiled no matter what," and then they both laugh.

"What," I say.

"Like...the poor people act spoiled, too," says the brunette, and the blonde one snickers and sips her vodka tonic through a straw.

"Entitled," she says.

The brunette one is drinking what I think is a gimlet. She takes a greedy gulp of it before following up with a haughty "yes" even though no one asked a question. I think they're really drunk. I laugh because I guess they're probably right and then I stare into space until they start talking again. I could try to be charming but I get the sense that there was never much of a chance that they'd be charmed by me.

One of them—the uglier one, the hot one moonlights as a model—eventually asks me what I do.

"Not much of anything really," I say. "But I'm...a writer."

They ooh and ahh and then the hot blonde one finds some guy who will buy them more drinks and they melt away from me.

"Sorry," someone whispers in my ear, and I flinch, but it's Tom. He sounded too loud to be him—he's normally very soft-spoken, but I guess maybe he's drunk.

"Sorry for what?"

"I thought this would be more fun," he says, trailing his hand down my shoulder and onto my back. It lingers where my waist starts to curve and I decide that he's definitely drunk.

"It's horrible," I say, and then I remember to laugh so I still seem like a good-time girl.

"Let's go," he says, and then I'm standing and we're walking toward the entrance. The pretty English girl is watching us go and I get the sense that she fucks Tom sometimes. I wonder if she knows he's emotionally unavailable; something tells me she probably does.

"I met some interesting people," I say, and he asks, "really?" and I say, "no, actually," and then giggle. We're outside now and it's freezing cold, too cold for October, but the city is loud and steaming and I rub my arms and Tom radiates heat and I don't feel cold anymore, not in my body.

"We'll get a cab," he says. He raises one eyebrow, which of course he can do.

"Where are we going?"

"Another party," he says, and then bumps into me teasingly. "No. We're going home."

"Isn't it close," I say.

"Yeah," he says, "but I'm trying to be a gentleman." I laugh and tell him he doesn't have to, not for me, and he was halfheartedly trying to hail a cab but he stops and we start to walk.

"I like walking," I say, and he says, "psycho." You would think that living in New York would necessitate a proclivity for walking, but I don't say that to him. His arm is brushing against the side of my body and he has a clean man smell, like the blue gel body wash that boys always have in their showers.

"A lot of those people seemed really annoying," I say, and he says, "oh, yeah." I wonder if all actors are narcissists and I imagine that not all the people in the bar were actors. They were definitely all narcissists, so maybe it's more of a square-rectangle thing. I once told Tom that I might like to be an actor because it seems like when you're an actor you get to do nothing all the time. He got really offended by that.

We walk quietly for a little bit and then he twists away and says fuck this and stumbles to the edge of the sidewalk to hail a cab. I bend over in laughter and say, "you're being so *opulent,*" and he says, "I don't feel like walking," and I can tell he's drunk but it's endearing because it's making him act more like he likes me without thinking about all the implications that go along with that kind of behavior.

Two cabs pass by and don't stop and he says fuck both times and I'm still laughing when he finally hails one down and sweeps his arm to gesture that I should go in first. I crawl into the cab before him and for a brief moment have the feeling that he's going to slam the door and run away, never to be seen again.

But of course he's climbing in after me and throwing his arm around my shoulders and authoritatively telling the driver where to go, which turns me on. We drive for a few minutes and he makes idle chitchat with the driver while drawing little circles on my bare shoulder under the sleeve of my t-shirt. Eventually they stop talking and he leans over and kisses my neck lightly and I had been staring out the window looking at the blinking lights which were so mesmerizing but I obligingly turn my head to kiss him.

When we get back to his place a few of his roommates are on the couch smoking weed and playing video games and we say hi but luckily not anything more than that and then we go to Tom's room. I ask for some water and he says yeah of course in the overpolite manner that guys have when they know they're about to get to fuck you.

He goes to the kitchen to get me water and I sit on his bed but then realize that I should take advantage of this time to explore his room and touch all his stuff. Before I can act on this impulse he's back and handing me a glass of water and then before I even have time to drink it he's rubbing the inside of my leg and trying to kiss me. I let him even though I'm thirsty. He's an okay kisser (hot guys are never amazing at sex) and he lies me down and takes my clothes off and says, "the female body is so beautiful," and we start to have sex slowly and uneventfully and it feels good but more because he's so hot and desirable and not necessarily because I'm turned on or desiring him in particular. I float up over my body and imagine that I'm watching myself having hot sex with this hot guy but even that is a little bit depressing. I'm thinking about it too much so I close my eyes and try to just breathe but then I feel like I'm at a yoga class.

I forgot to tell him that I'm not on birth control, not anymore. "Don't come in me," I say. He frowns. "Don't come in me," I repeat. He raises an eyebrow, but then he nods.

When it's over, we shower. Tom always showers, sometimes I do sometimes I don't, everybody has their weird little things and they're not always endearing.

When I wake up I think about whether I should spend the day with Tom or not. I could—I know he doesn't have any auditions or anything today, but also I know he probably has a deep need to be alone and very little desire to spend the day with some slut. But in his sleep he looks sweet and maybe it's just because we spent the night together but I'm feeling nostalgic and tender. It feels creepy to watch him sleep but I'm always the first one awake when I have a sleepover with someone which is why I don't do it that often.

Tom twitches but doesn't wake up. It's so unfair that boys' eyelashes are always curved and thick and perfect. His are also dark dark black and they make his eyes look even bluer. But not now, since his eyes are closed. I just know how blue they are.

Outside his window the clouds are thick and puffy and pure pure white like angel wings and I feel like I could lie here forever but only if I were alone. Tom's going to wake up soon and he's not a morning person, so I should leave.

"I'm going to leave soon," I whisper to him once he starts to stir. I imagine it's the sexiest thing I could have said to him.

He flings his arm over me and for a second I let my entire body curve into his and I breathe in the way he smells, like artificial coconut.

It's October but in bed with him and his coconut smell with the sky so-baby-blue it feels like summer. "You can stay," he says, but I can't tell if he means it and of course I have to assume he doesn't.

"I've gotta go somewhere," I say.

"How cryptic."

"A meeting," I whisper. "I have a meeting." I wonder if he knows it's a lie.

"About your writing?" He sounds very awake now.

"Yes."

"Oh," he says. "That's great."

"Yeah," I say, already extricating myself from his arms. I sit on the edge of the bed and feel around with my feet for my clothes. Already I'm shaking with little shivers from how cold it is outside the covers and I hope Tom isn't watching me quiver unattractively. I find my jeans and then I stand up to pull them on. Tom is curled in bed still and even though he's much bigger than me he looks very sweet like that, almost like a child. But his back is broad and rippled from going to the gym and having annoyingly perfect genes. "It was really good to see you," I say, gently pulling my shirt out from where it was lodged under my pillow. Tom's pillow, technically, but it was the one I used last night.

"Yeah," he mumbles. "See you soon."

* * *

When I get on the subway I don't feel like going back to Lucas'. I feel like going somewhere far far away, the end of the world but not the Montauk end of the world. So I decide to go to Coney Island. No one will be there because it's fall and also because it's Coney Island. It feels appropriately insane to make this decision and when I get on the train I feel like I am exactly where I'm supposed to be which is something that I rarely feel. The sun is leaking in through the train car windows and I'm going over the bridge and I can see the whole city. I guess I could move here if I love it so much and think it's so beautiful but also it feels too beautiful to belong to me.

There're only two other people here and it's a young couple and how sweet they are with each other is making me feel a little sick. The girl has pink hair and the boy is wearing a Bape sweatshirt and he's leaning his head on her shoulder and periodically nuzzling her neck.

I think about how Tom is a nice person but he'll never love me, which is kind of mean. I'm not someone who normally sleeps in places that aren't a bed but I lean my head back against the glass of the subway car and I think I do drift off for a while because the ride should have been over an hour but it felt like fifteen minutes.

On the boardwalk basically everything is closed except for a stand that sells overpriced seafood. I get calamari because I haven't eaten since before I got on the LIRR last night and I'm starting to feel like I'm going to pass out. It's unseasonably warm but not unpleasantly warm, and I eat the calamari at a chipped table that's the same light blue color as the clear sky. It tastes like seawater but rubbery and crispy and it's the best thing I've eaten in months.

I imagine that a hundred years ago or even fifty years ago it was probably a lot of fun to be here on a warm fall day. But now there are only homeless people and other weird loners like me and the people who work here. I think about how if I liked hot dogs I would get a hot dog, but I don't really like hot dogs. I do, I guess, because who wouldn't, but they feel like too gross and fatty of a junk food for me to eat.

I walk along the boardwalk and start to sweat even though I'm only wearing a t-shirt. I forgot my little cardigan at Tom's house and now he'll probably throw it away or give it to another girl and lie and tell her it's his sister's or something. I pass by a couple, a different one from the train, and the girl is wearing flip-flops and eating a hot dog. Her hair is blonde and looks wet even though it's dry. He has his hand in her back pocket and is wearing one of those DC hoodies that boys wore when I was in middle school in like 2012. I walk for maybe twenty minutes until I get overwhelmed and have to sit down. I press my palms into my eyes and feel them squish against each other until I see stars.

"Are you okay?" someone is asking me. I look up. It's an old man wearing fingerless gloves.

"I'm fine," I say. "Thanks." He doesn't move away from me so I repeat, "I'm fine," and he blinks.

"Do you have a cigarette?" he asks, and then he extends a gloved hand. The skin of his fingers that I can see above the gloves looks grey.

"No," I say, even though I do. "Sorry." Right after I say it I feel intensely guilty. I shouldn't even have cigarettes at all; I could have given him the whole pack without even thinking about them later. I only keep them because it's something to do with my hands sometimes. If one of the boys had asked I'm sure I would have given them away.

He blinks one more time and then backs away smiling.

"You're beautiful," he says, and then he turns around and walks toward the ocean. Then I really do start to cry, but the kind of crying where the tears just leak out of your eyes and you don't make any noise or understand why you're crying. It all feels very hormonal and I wonder if perhaps one of the boys I've been having unprotected sex with has impregnated me.

When I finish crying and get a grip the sky is turning a brown-tinged grey and I start to feel like I could just close my eyes and sleep here and that nothing bad would happen to me, that maybe nothing bad will happen to me ever again. I think what's actually happening is the calamari was not enough caloric intake and I'm still very hungry.

It starts to rain then, a type of rain that reminds me of Florida thunderstorms which I remember in a hazy child-hood-memory way even though I've only been to Florida a few times. They feel like a punishment from an angry God, and this time I look up at the sky and open my mouth until it fills with water and I choke a little bit. Then I decide that it's time to go home and eat something. Lucas' house home, not home home. I'll never go home home.

On my shuffling run-walk to the train the rain only gets worse. At one point through the lashing water I see a glassy-eyed young woman walk by. She looks past me but not at me. The rain doesn't seem to bother her at all and the streams on her face look like tears except she's smiling. I pass a mom and her kid jumping in puddles and laughing. When I get on the train I'm breathing very fast and shallow; I check my phone and there are no new messages.

Chapter Six

Lucas is in London for Halloween—I found this out from someone else. For some reason all I can think about when I think about London is that Smiths song where Morrisey whines about the double-decker bus running him over. And I don't even like the Smiths. I think I just want Lucas to get run over by a double-decker bus while he's in London, even though I know he won't. He'll probably have a great time and go to parties with lots of models and pretty girls who are otherwise employed in various useless industries. He loves girls like that; this is why he likes me. He's asked a million times to read the manuscript of my novel and I always say he can read it and then I never show it to him because I'd be embarrassed. Maybe if I did show it to him then the nature of our relationship would change. Probably it wouldn't, though. I bet he wouldn't even read it.

I don't really like London. I don't really like Long Island, either, or where I grew up, or most places I've been in the world. I think actually the problem is me and not the various beautiful and otherwise perfectly wonderful places.

Halloween morning on Long Island is grey and misty,

very London gothic, and I think that's what's making me fixate on Lucas, who I'm sure is not thinking about me at all and eating sushi in Camden for lunch with a bunch of girls who are much thinner than I am.

I make coffee and sit moodily on the couch drinking it and staring at the unbroken mass of grey sky out the windows. I try to read a book but my mind is too focused on male attention and my current lack of it.

It's strange how everything can matter so much and yet simultaneously it feels like nothing that's happening now matters at all. Eventually I'll be thirty and I won't think about this time in my life at all, except maybe to say, "oh, that was strange how I lived in that guy's house," and then I'll move on to talking about actual important things that happened in my life. Or maybe nothing important will ever happen in my life, and I'll live in Lucas' house forever, waiting for his parents to get back from the South of France or wherever it is that they are. I kind of feel like I'm trapped in a liminal purgatory where I won't age or change or grow at all, not that this is a bad thing. No new wrinkles. And no regressing, I guess. Maybe a little regressing. The problem is that I don't know what my real life is going to be like. When you're a reasonably smart reasonably attractive young person people love to tell you that your life is made up of infinite possibilities. But with every second and every decision an infinite number of these infinite possibilities is obliterated. The possibilities that feel the most concrete to me change on a given day, but I often think about becoming a teacher, or working for some magazine or something, like a character in a book, or maybe becoming somebody's wife and cooking and stressing about countertop materials. I am actually a very good cook, and the terrifying thing is that I could see myself becoming a person who has lots of things to say about the proper material for a kitchen island countertop, or bathroom tiles, or a car that's safe for children. But maybe this is all just an elaborate defense mechanism because what I really am, primarily, is terrified that I'll fail as an artist. Of course it's stupid to think of myself as an artist, I'm really trying to be a writer, but artist sounds much more sultry and glamorous. I always wished I could be a painter. Unfortunately, though, I can't really do anything. I can barely write. While I'm mulling all this over my coffee gets cold and the sky turns from grey to powder blue.

By noon I've been invited to a Halloween party at some guy's house in Sag Harbor, a guy I know from online. Cameron's not around, for once. I think he went into the city, but I'm not sure. When we're not physically together I think we kind of cease to exist to each other. Or at least I cease to exist for him. I've been thinking about him way too much but that's kind of normal for me. At least thinking about people in a deeply obsessive way is better than shooting heroin or committing a homicide. Marginally better, probably, but better.

I decide to go to the Halloween party even though I don't really know anyone there. I don't want to sit alone on Halloween and watch some movie like a loser, even though it would probably be a better use of my night to watch *Jennifer's Body* than to go sulk in a corner at some dumb party. I feel like being around people and I feel beautiful for once, so I want everyone to look at me even though I'm sure the second I get there I'll feel repulsive and want to leave. Plus this house is really scary alone at night. It always feels like some creature is out there, crouching in the shadows, waiting to eat me even though I don't actually belong here and it's not my house. In every one of my imagined scenarios where some murderer or monster breaks in, imaginary-me always screams no, wait, you've got the wrong person, even though of course whoever was attacking me wouldn't care whether it was my house or not.

The guy who invited me to the Halloween party is a lot older so I know he'll be happy to see me if only for my youth and charm. We've slept together only a few times because I think we both get a little freaked out by how much older he is, but this is a very normal and adult thing. Plenty of my more cosmopolitan friends have been sleeping with men in their fifties all through college, and psychologically they're not any worse off. That I know of.

I don't have a costume but I'm sure I could scrounge something from the rich people detritus around the house. Or there's always throwing on one of Lucas' blazers and saying I'm Patrick Bateman. That'll probably kill with the Hamptons crowd. Except I think the guy who invited me to his party runs some sort of artist's colony, so it might be more stoner-type art people than cocaine and finance.

I wonder what Lucas is dressing up as. If I had to put money on it, I'd say he probably doesn't even know that today is Halloween.

* * *

I get to the party and instantly realize I shouldn't have come. I don't know any of the people here and everyone is on drugs and smiling, which is freaking me out. I could either leave now in shame or get super drunk.

While I'm leaning on the wall and debating someone presses a bottle of white wine into my hand and introduces himself. Now that someone's given me wine I feel obligated to get super drunk. The wine-bringer is a filmmaker and he lives in East Hampton. The wine is awful and syrupy but I choke it down and listen to my new friend discuss the quality of the light on the beaches here; it's better than being by myself but not by much.

I ended up wearing a big blazer and a pair of headphones (Bateman, obviously), but no one's asked me what my costume is and I get the feeling that no one will. The filmmaker reaches inside my blazer's loose sleeve and runs a finger down my arm. The finger is cold and wet, either from wine bottle condensation or sweat. I start to feel nauseous but I make sure to smile and be sweet. It's always good to be a sweet girl.

After the filmmaker (whose costume I can't figure out —he's just wearing a Hawaiian shirt, I think) gets pulled away by a Playboy Bunny, I decide to hide in the bathroom. Or I should say I try to hide in the bathroom and someone who is either Dolly Parton or Anne Hathaway's character from *Brokeback Mountain* is doing cocaine off the marble sink with Edward Scissorhands. The bathroom smells like the inside of a Nutter Butter and also mold. "Oh," says Dolly/Anne. "Do you want some?" I shake my head and wander from the bathroom into the hallway. There's a spiral staircase across the room, dotted with people, but I assume there's probably another bathroom upstairs.

I wander up the stairs and brush past Shego and two angels. One of the angels is very pretty. The upstairs is dimly lit and heavily carpeted. It's one of those white furry carpets that I can tell is soft even though I have shoes on. I wonder how the carpet stays so white, since everyone in here seems to be wearing shoes. Maybe everyone's shoes are clean. Except for mine. There's a purple door and I press it open gently. It's a bedroom. Then a yellow-ish door, also a bedroom, then two white ones. All bedrooms, all empty. I've never been in a house with so many bedrooms in a row. The next door is purple again. I open it and see the Playboy Bunny with her legs splayed on the California King and a flash of orange from the filmmaker's Hawaiian shirt while he's giving her head. Sweat slicks his hair to the back of his neck and neither of them looks like they're having a good time. The filmmaker stops but doesn't notice me right away. Bunny does, though.

"Do you want to join?" she asks, and from this distance it looks like her eyes are all pupil.

"I would...prefer not to," I say, and then I click the door shut and feel stupid for saying no like that. I bet that's where the bathroom was. In my opinion it's bad manners to fuck in the master bedroom at someone's house party, but what do I know about manners. I'm drunk. I look at the closed door and wish that Cameron was here. I wish I hadn't left him last week to go into the city and see Tom. If Cameron had been here tonight I would have stayed with him.

* * *

Everyone starts to leave and I wonder whether I should go but I'm too fucked up to drive still and there's no goddamn Uber in the Hamptons. I guess I could ask for a ride but I don't think any one of these people knows me well enough to say yes and I don't think they're sober enough to drive either. Also I don't want to have to come back here and pick up the car later.

I end up scrolling through Instagram on the couch feeling awkward and terrible and then the guy who invited me here comes up to me and sighs and says, "come with me," like he's resigning himself to this. I guess I was probably not his first-choice girl. But I am the girl who's still around and he leads me up the stairs to a narrow hallway with a skylight, a part of the house I didn't see when I was upstairs before, and I think about how everyone out here is so in love with their fucking skylights, and then we go into a bedroom where everything is white and thank God I'm not on my period. I mean *everything* is white, like that riddle where there's a house where everything is purple but it's a one-story house so there's no purple stairs. Not anything in the room is another color. It almost feels fake, like heaven or I guess not like heaven but like some other place where everything is white. I sit down on the bed and then he looks at me like he's about to tell me I'm going to get it dirty. He doesn't say anything, he just takes off his shoes and then walks into the closet. I'm not sure what he's doing in there but I hear shuffling noises and when he comes out he's wearing just boxers and a t-shirt. I guess he was probably changing. He sits next to me and I think about asking him something but I wait for him to say something first and he doesn't, he just reaches his hand out to pull me into him and then we're kissing. I guess it's easier when you cut out the talking part.

We take off all our clothes and he asks if he can fuck me from behind and I say I don't like it like that. "Why not?" he asks. "You have the perfect body for it."

I say it makes me feel slutty.

"But you are slutty," he says, turning me around. "You're a fuckin' whore." And when he starts moving I hate how good it feels and I hate myself for liking it and breathing hard and saying "mhm" to him when he asks "yeah" like it's a question. He starts moving faster and all I can think about is whether the bedroom the Playboy Bunny was getting head in was the master, or if it's this one.

When it's over he falls asleep right away and I guess he was pretty drunk, way too drunk for Halloween, in my humble opinion. I think about how he called me a whore and about how I kind of am one. Every woman is, really, and it's very big of me that I can at least admit that I am. It's obvious for me with Lucas and the house and all but for a lot of my friends it's less obvious. They let guys take them out and buy them drinks and sometimes pay for other things and it's easy to think that this is just niceness, just the way things are, but really it makes you a whore. The best thing you can do is be intentional about it. But a good whore should take care of herself, look good, etc., and I don't. I haven't had my nails done since graduation. It feels like everything that's happened since then could have happened over the course of a week. Or ten years. Maybe I just feel like I've aged ten years. I'm such an aimless-spoiled-graduate cliché and I'm making myself sick. The only reason I keep doing stupid bullshit like fucking some loser at a Halloween party is so that I don't have to think like this.

While I'm thinking these lucid thoughts and the man next to me snores it occurs to me that the sex made me sober enough to drive. I weigh whether staying and not getting any sleep is worth the potential of getting to fuck this guy again later in the morning. I decide it's not. I get up and leave my clothes on the floor except for Lucas' blazer even though I'm sure he would never notice it was gone. On my way out I steal a pair of this guy's jeans (a pair that looks expensive enough to justify the theft but not so expensive that he'll notice they're missing—I'm not an idiot).

There are people crashing on the couch, some guy and a painter girl who I met briefly last night and thought was really pretty. Her tits are out and her angel wings are crushed on the floor and covered in something sludgy and brown. The wings are coated in iridescent sequins and they look painstakingly handmade. I wonder if the painter girl will be upset that they're ruined.

A few people are awake in the kitchen murmuring in dulcet tones and probably making coffee. If I weren't such a miserable freak I'd go talk to them, maybe have some coffee, but of course I creep out while trying to make as little noise as possible. I'd love to be one of those girls who can show up at a party and charm everyone and appear instantly comfortable, but I'm not. Instead I feel like someone is about to ask me to leave. But I always feel like that.

I walk outside to the car and in the silvery morning light this guy's house looks smaller but more terrifying, like the big white house in *Funny Games* (the one with Naomi Watts, obviously). The grass is a lurid green and someone vomited next to the brittle carcasses of the dead hydrangeas. The morning air smells sour like vomit but also clear and sweet like fall. My stomach hurts and I realize that I'm probably hungry and that I should stop somewhere on the way back. I want something greasy like an egg sandwich but I know that I'd probably end up throwing that up.

I pull out of the circular driveway, and for a second I feel more alone than I've ever felt. Even though I'm wearing fancy new jeans I think about how if I were a person who regretted things then this Halloween party might be something I regret.

Chapter Seven

It's solidly November now and I'm in the kitchen making a depressing stir-fry with stale rice from Cameron's take-out. He got back from the city a few days ago and I've kind of settled into the fact that he's just living here, too. We're both just living here, in Lucas' house, without Lucas. It's the kind of thing my friends don't understand when I try to explain it to them over FaceTime.

I don't think I'm going to share the rice with Cameron even though it's his rice. He went out a few hours ago and he's not back and I don't know where he is.

I sit down at the kitchen counter and stare at the Word document with my manuscript and shovel the rice into my mouth. The only thing I can think to write about is myself.

I put egg in the rice and I don't think the egg is all the way cooked so it tastes raw and wet. Hopefully I'll get salmonella and die without ever finishing any of my projects so that everyone can say I was a genius with infinite potential.

I hear someone fiddling with the lock and I assume it's Cameron back from wherever-the-fuck and then it is and it's also Lucas and they're laughing about something and I'm choking on my rice. It feels like an individual grain is lodged in my trachea or windpipe or wherever air comes in and tears are streaming down my face and Cameron asks, "you alright?" and I just cough and hold up my hand. "Is that my rice?" he asks. I can feel Lucas looking at me and I don't know which of them to look at. I land on looking at neither of them; instead I stare at a yolky grain of rice that sits in a cloudy yellow puddle on the table and think about what a gross mess I am.

"I didn't know you were coming," I say to Lucas. I dart my eyes back and forth between the two of them and even though I think of Cameron as being so much taller they're actually about the same height.

"I thought I said I was going to get him," Cameron says, and now I know to focus on him and say, "no, no, you didn't," very neutrally. Lucas stares at me impassively and Cameron stares at me impassively. I get the sense that Cameron is mildly uncomfortable and Lucas is maybe enjoying himself, but maybe I'm projecting because of the way I think about each of them.

"I bought a Nespresso," Lucas says, and he puts the massive hunk of metal that he was carrying down on the counter. I assumed it was some sort of scrap thing for an art project that he picked up at the dump or just some shit a girl gave him or something. But I guess it is too shiny and new for that.

"The coffee machine thing," I say, reaching out a finger to see if it feels as shiny as it looks. It does. I've never seen one before and I wonder if he brought one here because he's planning to be here for a long time or if it's just the kind of weird shit that he'd buy because he's got money. Could be either one. I look at the other fancy coffee machine that's already on the counter. I never figured out how to use it and now I never have to.

"What should we have for dinner," Lucas asks.

"We could order pizza," Cameron says. "She's a good cook," he adds, like I'm not in the room.

"Yeah, I know," Lucas says, even though I've never cooked with or for him. I get the sense that these two boys are competing about property ownership and that it has nothing to do with me.

"How was London?" I ask Lucas, and he gives a wolfish smile that I know means he had a brilliant sexy time and that he'll never tell me about it because he likes to cultivate mystery and intrigue.

"Oh yeah, you were in London," Cameron says. Cameron is half-English which is why he's so pale and probably also why he's such a fucking asshole. My mom always says that the English want to make everyone else as miserable as they are.

"It was good," Lucas says. He doesn't look at either of us; he just spins a packet of rolling papers on the marble countertop.

"Should we, should we...eat or something?" Cameron asks. He's rolling a j and trying to affect nonchalance but I can tell by his tone that he's forcing things.

"I'll make dinner," I say. "I can make salmon. And, like, potatoes and shit."

"Yeah?"

"Cool." They shift back and forth and then Lucas fixes me with his big scary eyes. Cameron won't look at me. "We'll go to the shop. Since you're gonna cook."

"I can go," I say.

"Nah, it's alright. You'll come, yeah," Lucas nudges Cameron and then Cameron nods.

"Okay," I say, and then I look at the pure tooth-white of

the countertop. I think about how now they've both fucked me on it. "I'm gonna go for a swim," I say.

"But it's freezing," Cameron says, looking at me for the first time since they walked in. His expression is entirely unreadable. Either that or I'm just bad at reading it.

"I feel like a swim," I say, and Lucas laughs.

"Yeah. Right."

They start off toward Lucas' room, chatting quietly about some band they're both into that Lucas saw in London and I've never heard of.

I wait until I hear them both leave for the store, because I want to swim naked.

The pool feels colder than last time but still nice, and the bracing unpleasantness is almost the perfect feeling, probably because I feel like I deserve to be shivering and wet and doused in icy saltwater. I don't know why the pool's still open in November, but Lucas hasn't mentioned anything about it to me. He probably expects me to close it. I think if I tried I would probably get wrapped up in the bird-shit-encrusted pool cover and drown. Actually, that would be a pretty poetic way to go. Maybe at dinner tonight I'll offer to close it up.

There's a scummy layer of leaves on top of most of the pool. It's been weeks since I skimmed it with the little net. I think Cameron might have fished out a drowned bird or two, but I'm not sure. All I know is they were there and then they weren't. I wonder briefly if there's bacteria in the water from the leaves and the birds and the stagnancy but I bet it's so cold that it doesn't matter. And also if I get sick from a brain-eating amoeba and die then maybe I'll find out if anyone really cares about me.

For some reason the dead leaves are all clustered at the deep end and when I swim through them the light is filtered and spins out in fractals through the water. I keep my eyes open until they start to burn from the salt and then I squeeze them shut, but the patterns of light are burned in purple on the inside of my lids. It feels so beautiful to be alone, but also I remember what it was like that first night I was here when Lucas and I swam naked together and it still felt like summer. I think I only remember it so fondly because I'm the type of person who romanticizes things in retrospect. Not exactly nostalgic, because I'm not old, but maybe wistful. The only time I can enjoy things is when I'm remembering them. Now, under the water, I open my eyes. I think about how all the times I've been in this pool are happening right now, all at once. It's quiet and still in here but too cold to feel womblike or safe.

I wish Cameron were in here with me or even Lucas and with both of them here it's impossible that either of them will touch me. If they were threesome-type guys then maybe I'd be worried or excited, but they're both so anxious and internal that I don't think they'd ever make it happen even if they wanted to.

I get out of the pool and immediately my skin erupts in angry goosebumps. I run inside with a towel thrown loosely around my body and then I take a hot hot shower. I burn myself clean and I emerge fresher and newer than if neither of them had ever touched me. I put on all white: my favorite white pants and a tight white tank top. My skin is raw and pinkish.

There are three brown bags crumpled on the kitchen counter. I see the bags before I see Cameron and Lucas because the boys somehow blend in naturally with the house, like they belong there. Which I guess they do.

"How was the swim?" Cameron asks.

"It was good," I say. I can feel the cold water from my wet hair pooling on my neck and in the hollow of my collarbone. It's funny how the water in a hot shower is so scalding at first but then instantly becomes freezing once it's been in contact with skin for longer than a few seconds. Because skin is warm.

Cameron blinks at me. He is probably waiting for me to say more than just it was good and I open my mouth to say something about the leaves when he cuts me off. "Are you, um, are you cold?"

"No," I say, and then I realize that I am. Lucas is frowning at his phone and either not paying attention to us or doing a great job of pretending to not be paying attention to us.

"You look cold," he says. I look at him for a long time, probably too long, and then I walk out of the room. In the bedroom—I do normally think of it as my bedroom, but with Lucas here it feels more appropriate to say the bedroom—I press my palms into the wrought iron knobs on the dresser but it doesn't hurt like I want it to and so I stop.

I take a sweater from the pile on the floor and then I rethink putting it on because it'll make me look worse. I'm cold but not so cold that I don't care about looking beauti-ful. I haven't seen Lucas in so long and he hardly seems to care whether I'm here or not. It's almost as though he forgot I was staying here. Which I guess could be the case. I drape the sweater over my shoulders like a shawl and make sure a creamy expanse of skin is still visible. I adjust my necklace so my silver cross sits right at the hollow of my chest and then I slap my cheeks quickly and lightly to make me look flushed and pink. The pink of my cheeks and the white of my clothes and the tarnished silver of the cross make me feel good. I could see how someone could maybe desire me.

Maybe I'll get drunk with the boys. If I get drunk I'll feel even prettier. And I can stop thinking about how Lucas maybe doesn't care about me. Or only cares about me when I'm right in front of him.

When I come back out the boys are staring at each other listlessly. I always wonder whether boys are friends because they actually like each other or whether it's mostly situational for them. Most of the boys I know are friends because they were roommates or something.

Lucas turns on music from his laptop and then Cameron says, "I have a speaker," and Lucas nods. Cameron goes to get his speaker and then Lucas and I are alone for the first time since August. I don't look at him. Instead I chop tri-color potatoes in half and put them in a glass Pyrex. Dinner's going to be really good and I almost wish I were making it for different people, but I can't think of any different people I would cook for. "Um," I say, and then Cameron comes back with the speaker and then they're blasting Yung Lean and Lucas is pulling out a handle of fancy-looking gin that he presumably brought from London. Instead of making us all drinks he screws the top off and takes a swig right from the bottle.

"Straight gin," I say, and then I stick my tongue out a little bit and scrunch up my mouth. I immediately regret talking and sounding like a fucking mom but Cameron laughs.

"It's kinda good, actually," Cameron says after taking a drink.

"Here." Lucas grabs the bottle back from him and then walks it over to me. Our hands brush when he passes the bottle to me and his skin is so dry that it doesn't even feel like skin. After he hands me the bottle he stays standing next to me, close enough that it's not quite normal. I drink the gin and Lucas looks at my throat while I swallow.

"It's good," I say, even though it's not. I could see how someone could think it was good.

Lucas doesn't move away from me, so I start shaving garlic to add to the steamed broccoli and potatoes and eventually he walks back over to sit with Cameron. Lucas asks if I want help and then Cameron offers too, but I can tell neither of them really feels like helping me, or if they do it's only because they think that's how they're supposed to feel.

I say it's fine, everything's easy, and I let them keep drinking and laughing softly to each other. I can hear the cadences of their speech but I can't really make out individual words. I let it wash over me while I chop the garlic. The repetitive motion is very soothing and for a second I'm reminded of the only time I've gone to the beach since I came out here. It was after Lucas left and before Cameron got here. The waves were huge and crashing because of a storm further North, and when I got out of the water my hands shook and I cried.

Cameron is rifling through the refrigerator now and my stomach feels warm from the gin. I probably shouldn't have had any; hard liquor makes me disagreeable.

"Do you want one?" Cameron asks. He's near my ear and he speaks loud enough for me to hear but quiet enough for Lucas not to. He hands me a beer even though I don't confirm that I want it. Lucas is looking at us, his icy eyes wide. But they're always wide. "Are you sure you don't need help?" Cameron asks, this time so that Lucas can hear.

"No," I say. "I just have to put these in the oven, then I'll sit."

I sprinkle thyme and rosemary over the potatoes. The boys bought everything from the store that I asked for, which was a surprise. I wonder if they knew what rosemary and thyme looked like or if they had to ask. I know Cameron wouldn't have known but somehow I can't picture them asking anyone either. Maybe Lucas knew.

After I put the potatoes in the oven I quickly mix mustard and brown sugar for the salmon glaze.

"Do you want to taste it?" I ask. I don't address the question to either of them. Cameron gets up right away but Lucas doesn't. He smiles benevolently and gestures for Cameron to try it. I wonder if Cameron felt like he needed Lucas' permission. "Tell me if it needs more sugar," I say. I hand him a clean spoon and it's cold in my hand but now I'm not cold, I'm very warm, maybe because I'm so close to the oven. I take my sweater and drape it over a chair while Cameron is tasting.

"It's good," he says. "Maybe a little more sugar."

I nod and then dip my finger in. I probably should have used a spoon and I can feel my cheeks getting hot. I lick my finger and then press the bottle of beer Cameron gave me into my neck. The boys are watching me and my hands are trembling slightly when I take the chopped broccoli and put it in the pot with some garlic to steam later.

"I'll sit," I say. "The potatoes are going to need a while."

Lucas smiles and pats the empty space next to him. I sit on the couch and I can feel my body start to curve to be closer to his, not because I want it to. I wish I could control it, could control anything. Lucas reaches over and carelessly rubs a strand of my hair between his thumb and forefinger. "You're very wet still," he says. I smile. I can feel Cameron watching us even though he's pretending to drink beer and look at his phone. The music that's playing is Lucas' music. I think it's The Cure but I'm not positive. F-i-r-e i-n C-a-i-r-o. I love music but not in any real way. I mostly listen to whatever it is boys decide to play for me.

"Alright," I say. I smile big and lean in toward the exact geometric centerpoint between the three of us. I've decided it's time to be brilliant and charming. "Can I ask you guys something?" They look a little freaked out but I smile and take a sip of my drink and then smile again slowly and smugly this time so they know nothing's wrong. "Would you rather live in a beautiful building overlooking an ugly building, or an ugly building overlooking a beautiful building?" I know they've never seen *Girls* so they won't know that this is where I know this question from. It's embarrassing to ask it, but I still think it's an important thing to know about people. And no one was talking. It's easier when there's talking. When I don't talk, they look at me like they're not sure why I'm there.

"The beautiful building," Lucas says right away. I knew he would say this but I wasn't sure he'd say it so quickly. Cameron thinks for a long time and sips his beer. I can see him wanting to disagree with Lucas but I think he knows that the beautiful building is the right answer.

"Yeah," he finally says. "The beautiful building."

I throw my head back and laugh and for a moment I feel really truly happy. "Of course," I say. "That's the right answer."

"I guess it'd be nice to have a good view," Lucas says. I can tell he's in a rare mood. Normally he stares into space and doesn't say much.

"Okay," I say. "How about this one." They both look at me and it feels so good to have their eyes on my skin even though I know this is all so unsustainable.

"You're at a family member's funeral, and—"

"Which family member," Lucas says.

"I don't know," I say. "Your dad, maybe. It doesn't matter."

"Okay," Cameron says.

"Okay," I say. "And you see the most beautiful girl you've ever met. And you hit it off. Like, she's perfect for you, and you talk the whole time. And then you go to get some drinks and when you come back, she's gone." Lucas is frowning but I can tell he's kind of stopped listening. Cameron's eyes are wide and his gaze is blank but he's looking right at me and I know he's paying attention. "How do you make sure you can see her again?"

"I don't know," Lucas says.

"You can't," Cameron says. "You probably never will." He's looking at the wall now instead of me and his eyes aren't as wide as they were. He gave the same answer I did when I first heard the riddle.

"You could kill someone else in your family," Lucas says. His drink is gone but he's running his finger gingerly around the lip of the glass. His nails are jagged and bitten. I want to file them. "Like, someone in the dead person's immediate family. Because she'd probably come to that funeral, too." So he was listening. I didn't think he was.

"Oh," Cameron says. "That's probably the right answer." He's looking right at me and I know he wants to know how I can let Lucas be so cruel to me, how I can let someone so cruel touch me and control me and do what he wants to me, or maybe he's just stoned and drunk and not thinking this at all and only looking at me because I'm pretty or even just because I'm in his line of sight. Lucas is watching him watch me and I am careful to keep my face entirely impassive.

Lucas knows me and I know he probably assumes that something has happened or is happening with me and Cameron. I just can't tell whether that bothers him or not. Generally he's the most unbothered person I've ever known, but I imagine him being bothered would manifest itself in some sort of situation that would not be very pleasant for me.

"Yeah," I say. "It is." Lucas smiles without crinkling his eyes and I say, "people don't usually get that one right." Cameron gets up for a beer and asks if either of us wants one. The heavy chrome of the fridge door muffles his voice and cuts off his head so that his body looks headless and illuminated from the pure white glow of the fridge's interior.

"Sure," I say. It's hard to eat in front of the boys but it's fine to drink. "I should...I should check on everything." I feel like a 50's housewife, and I don't even necessarily hate it. I wonder if 50's housewives were drunk all the time. Probably they were. It seems to be the only thing that helps.

I shake the potatoes a little bit when I open the oven. They're getting close to being ready, so I take the brush from where I left it on the counter and the broccoli and salmon from where I put them in the fridge. Cooking, I imagine, is the same as open-heart surgery. You have to be very careful to get everything right or the entire thing goes to shit incredibly quickly. I make sure to distribute the glaze exactly evenly between the three pieces of salmon. They're huge hunks of meat, pink and glistening and shot through with white ropes of fat. I wouldn't have picked ones like this.

"How hungry are you guys?" I ask. I hear my voice from far away, like it's the voice of a woman on TV speaking to her family. For a second I flicker in and out of my body and I can see myself bending over the oven and inspecting the salmon glaze.

"Starving," Cameron says. Lucas says nothing.

"I'm hungry, too," I say. Cameron stands up and gets more beer from the fridge. He opens one and puts it on the counter next to me even though I still have about a quarter left of the last one. But why drink the lukewarm dregs of an old beer when you could have the nose-fizzing ice-cold beginning of a new one. I guess that's the question.

"It smells good," Lucas says.

The boys start talking about music, again, and I look

out the window at the glow of the moon. The light is pearly and silver.

I take everything off the heat at the perfect time. "It's ready," I say. They both say thank you and get up to serve themselves. I go between Lucas and Cameron and I spoon my food carefully, so that none of it touches and all the colors have their separate corners against the white of the plate. It looks the way fake food looks in advertisements. The boys heap everything on top of everything else. Cameron takes most of the salmon and Lucas, surprisingly, takes a mountain of broccoli. I never thought of him as someone who would eat vegetables but I guess people can always surprise you.

We eat basically in silence, probably because everyone's tipping past bubbly drunk and into sleeping drunk, and because we used up all our conversation earlier. I did, anyway. The salmon is wet and salty and it melts apart on my tongue. Even the broccoli is good. It's probably the best thing I've ever cooked. The boys eat quickly, like they can't even taste it. At one point Lucas suggests watching a movie and Cameron makes an assenting noise but no one moves to turn anything on. The sauce from the salmon runs into the juice from the broccoli on my plate and it makes me think about how behind the thin layer of my skin my body is basically made of only fluid.

"I'm going to go to bed," I finally say, and the boys both look at me and jerk their heads a little but they don't say anything. I think we're all blind drunk and even if we weren't I don't know if they'd care. They'd sit there all night staring at each other whether I was there or not, I think. I wish I could take food and eat it alone in my room without them watching me. In front of them I could only push it around my plate and take a few small bites. Mostly I drank the beer and thought about how my mouth tasted like ash no matter how much food or liquid I put in it.

In the bedroom I drink three glasses of water and swish wet toothpaste around my mouth because I'm too drunk to brush my teeth. In the mirror I look beautiful and perfect except for my bloodshot eyes. If I were anyone else I think seeing the boys like this could have been fun, or even made me happy.

* * *

Lucas comes into my room at two in the morning and wakes me up. He doesn't ask if he can; he just gets into bed with me. But it's his bed, in his house, so I let him. I'm sleepy and still drunk enough to feel foggy, so when he reaches for me I reach back and we meet somewhere in the middle. Then we're wrapped around each other and he tastes like cigarettes and I wonder if they're his or Cameron's but I can't taste the difference between an American Spirit mouth and a whatever-the-fuck-it-is-that-Lucas-uses-mouth.

He's unbuttoning his pants and then reaching for mine and he inhales and murmurs, "we shouldn't," and I do nothing, say nothing. We both breathe in the blue quiet and then he says, "I have a girlfriend." To which I do nothing except blink a few times. "Okay," I say. Neither of us moves away from each other and he's tracing little circles on my arm with his finger which doesn't seem like the type of thing you do if you're in love with your girlfriend. But Lucas is kind of a sociopath and I don't think he's capable of being in real love with someone who loves him back, uncomplicatedly. Not that I know anything about his girlfriend or their relationship.

"She lives in the city," he says. "But she's from London." In what world he thinks it's appropriate to talk about his girlfriend while one of his hands is still absentmindedly fiddling with the waistband of my underwear I'll never be sure. "But I want you," he says quietly, almost to himself, and I turn around so we're not facing each other and press my body into his. For a while his shallow breathing gets deeper and I think he might be falling asleep but he's moving against me and I'm breathing deeper too and not falling asleep.

"I really want to fuck you," he says.

"Why?"

"I don't...what do you mean, why?"

"Because you're attracted to me physically?" I ask. "Or because of my personality?"

"I don't know," he says. At this point I've turned around to face him and his ice-chip blue eyes are focused on some point beyond my face. He seems to really be thinking about something, but I don't think it's my question. "Both, I guess." I can't decide whether to believe him or whether it even matters. I turn back around and he starts to move against me and I kind of feel like it only feels this delicious because we're not going to have sex, and I don't really even want to, either, because of Cameron and because Lucas has a girlfriend. Not that I care about the girlfriend or anything, I just care about being a second choice. But maybe I'm not a second choice, since here I am, in his house. I'm a different choice, I guess. But still I'd never be his girlfriend, or at least he's never given me any sign that he would want that. And I think it's because he knows I might not want it. Maybe I'm an idiot but maybe I'm also smart, too smart to be someone's girlfriend. Thinking that makes me feel better even though I don't believe it.

Lucas is still grinding his body into mine and breathing into my ear and I'm sighing because no matter the emotional consequence it's of course always nice to have someone touch you and desire you so obviously. He pulls away to get a condom from where I know he keeps them in the pocket of his jeans, and I think the moment we lose contact the spell kind of breaks because when he lies back down he doesn't touch me. He's staring at the ceiling now and so am I and I wonder how it is that he's the one who came in here and now he gets to be the one who decides we're not doing this. I prop myself on my elbow to look at him but a few minutes go by and he doesn't look at me so I go back to staring at the ceiling.

"You believe in God, right?" Lucas finally says, and I nod. He reaches for my neck and gently fingers the chain that my cross is on. He doesn't touch the cross, just the chain.

"And aren't you into Satan and shit?" I say.

"Yeah," he says, and his hand moves back down over my hip and thigh. "You seem too smart to believe in God."

"Well, I'm not really that smart." I lean on my side again so I can look at him and I see his eyelids flutter a little bit. "I just have a good memory." He smiles and now he's finally looking at me. He traces the line of my ribs with his dry lizard skin hands and then I think he starts to fall asleep. I'll never understand how boys can fall asleep in situations like this because I feel like I'm on fire and I'm pissed off at him for not having sex with me which I know is bad, but still I feel like he should've at least fingered me a little.

I know Lucas only came in here to reclaim ownership of me from Cameron, but I don't care. It's alright being something that people treat like an object, in fact it's kind of fun, and I know it's not going to stay like this forever so I'm just going to enjoy it while I can. Lucas is snoring softly next to me and it feels warmer in the bed now that he's here and I know when I wake up I'm not going to feel hungover because for once I'm going to sleep well.

Cameron

When I wake up I go out to smoke and I can see her through her window. She's on the bed, lying on top of the covers in a sweatshirt and underwear. Lucas' jeans are crumpled by her head.

I stand by the pool for a while and just look at her lying there, almost like she's dead. I don't even think she's sleeping. She's just staring into space, not moving at all. If she knew I was watching her I think she would be really upset. But I don't watch her for that long, or maybe I do. She looks really pretty like that which I know is kind of fucked up but it's true, she really does. I can see the spot in the garden where some of the roses were flattened from when I ran over to her while her hands bled, even though that feels like so long ago now. Something I'm realizing is that you can have sex with someone and it doesn't mean you know them any better than before you had sex with them. And now I'm realizing that this is the kind of thought she might have. I finish my cigarette and grind it out near the rosebushes where I guess someone, probably her, will eventually have to pick it up.

Chapter Eight

In the morning Lucas is gone, of course, and I'm the first one up, and also of course I don't know how to use the fucking Nespresso. I figure it can't be rocket science so I go over to where it stands gleaming on the counter, taunting me. It's too beautiful an object for what it is and I scowl at it like it has feelings and can read my facial expression.

"Fuck you," I say to it, and then I press what looks like a button but apparently is not. I jam a lever that seems like it might open the top hatch, but I only seem to damage the machine. The lever is now stuck at the halfway point and the little sleeves of purple and gold and metallic green pods are stacked in a neat little pyramid.

"Morning." Lucas is a terrible morning person, which I know because he normally slips away or kicks me out somehow by morning. The few times I've seen him before four PM he's dark-circled and scowling. There is something endearing about it, though.

"Morning." I smile wide and it's only partly a performance. The morning is my favorite part of the day. Before the day actually happens and ruins my mood.

"Do you need help?" he asks, smirking.

"With this thing?" I say. "They make it so easy to use."

He comes over and blocks my view of the controls with his body. I can't see how he does it but within ten seconds a thin steaming jet of liquid squirts out of the machine. I watch it hiss into the mug. Lucas is using the pink mug shaped like a pig that I never use because I think it's creepy.

"What do you want?" he asks.

"I don't...what do the colors mean?"

He points to the one he used. "Black coffee." Then he gestures to the green, then the silver, then the burnt golden-yellow. "Vanilla, espresso, and...latte, I think. I'm not sure."

"I don't care," I say. He makes me the same thing as his and puts it in the Proud Republican mug. I get oat milk from the fridge but Lucas waves it away when I offer it. I watch the white oaty cream mushroom out in my Nespresso and I wonder if maybe I am a little hungover.

"You look pretty," Lucas says, and my instinct is to look around and see who he's talking to even though obviously no one else is here.

"Thanks," I say. I wonder if he's making fun of me, but he would have no reason to do that. Maybe I do look pretty.

"Yeah," he says. "You do." He sips the coffee and watches me and all I can think about is when Cameron will wake up and save me from being alone with Lucas, who watches me like I'm a bug with a particularly interesting pattern on my tiny back.

* * *

After the coffee Lucas fucked off to God-knows-where and Cameron woke up, made a Nespresso, then went to his room to blast music. I guess everyone except me knows how to use that fucking thing.

I do wonder where Lucas slept last night after he left my room. There's another guest room but it only has two tiny twin beds and I can't imagine Lucas sleeping in a twin bed. I could go check and see if the bed looks slept-in, but that would require leaving the couch. On the couch I'm safe. On the couch I pretend to read and everyone can see me through the windows and I look like a normal girl reading in a normal Hamptons house. On the counter there's a Nespresso and in the bedroom there's a boy. No one would think that I'm too young and ugly to own property. Or that most people in my generation will never be able to own a house. This is the Hamptons and no one would think that because everyone has a trust fund. I decide that I *am* hungover and give up on pretending to read. I arrange myself on the couch prettily and close my eyes, imagining that when one of the boys sees me like this he'll think I'm the most beautiful girl in the world.

Of course, when I wake up, the side of my mouth is sticky with drool and my eyes are gummy with sleep. Also no one's watching me. I wonder if either of the boys saw me sleeping at all. Probably better if they didn't. There's something naked about how defenseless people are while they're sleeping, like they're suddenly a child. Or an animal.

The light from outside is dim now and the sun is setting so early. It's only six and it's almost pitch dark.

"Hey," Lucas says. "You're up."

"Oh," I say. "Fuck." He was at the kitchen table doing something on his computer. So I guess someone was watching me sleep.

"Cameron went out for burritos," he says.

"Oh," I say. "From that place."

"Yeah," Lucas says, smiling. "From *that* place."

I'm disoriented with sleep but I think even if I weren't I

wouldn't be able to tell whether he's mocking me or not. I can never tell.

"This is the only place in the world I can nap," I say. I twist my body around on the couch in a way that I hope is appealing. Lucas is looking at his phone.

"Really," he says. It sounds like what he wants to say is "stop talking." I sit and stare at the wall for a second. I imagine I can see Lucas' hands moving over the keyboard out of the corner of my eye. I can't, of course. I can only hear it. But I can trick my brain into thinking I can see him, now and all the time.

Keys jingle in the doorknob and it's such a comfortable domestic sound that for a second I feel like a little kid again, on school vacation for Christmas even though it's only November.

"Oh," Cameron says, pushing the door open. "She's awake." He's holding a grease-stained paper bag from the place and I wonder who paid for the burritos. Lucas, almost certainly. Or maybe Cameron. He's always broke until he's not.

Lucas says nothing, just wordlessly accepts the bag from Cameron and starts peeling the thin silver layer away from the burrito. They're the shrimp kind, of course, with extra special sauce. It smells like heaven even though I am, obviously, in hell.

Lucas hands me my burrito next and then Cameron gets his and we all silently listen to each other's wet chewing noises for a while. I don't even care that I'm eating in front of them. I'm still groggy and the burrito's so good and I feel like I haven't eaten properly in days or maybe weeks.

"Jacob's having a party," Lucas says, and it takes me a few seconds to remember who Jacob is. He's a rich kid from New York who's still at Oberlin or Bennington or one of those types of places. He looks a bit like Lucas if Lucas were miserable and tired. But I remember that he was nice and that we almost slept with each other.

Cameron smiles. "Jacob's great," he says.

"Why is he having a party?" I ask.

"I don't know," Lucas says. "But let's go in like an hour."

Cameron nods and disappears into the back room. I stare at Lucas for what feels like a full minute and eventually he offers me a puff of a j that seems to have materialized out of nowhere even though he was probably smoking it this whole time.

* * *

We get to the party and everyone looks old and tired. I guess we were seventeen and eighteen when we last saw each other, and some of these people even looked bad then. Lucas and Cameron are the only ones who look better.

Jacob used to throw a party every long weekend back in high school and every time someone almost died. I wonder if anyone will die tonight, now that we're older and probably more likely to die anyway.

It's a Friday night and I made the mistake of telling my mom over the phone earlier that Lucas was taking me to a party in the city because I thought it would make me seem like more of a normal person. She told me to make sure I remembered to put on mascara. She always says I look so much better with a little bit of makeup on.

I put on mascara and a mesh shirt like a little fool and now I feel like I tried too hard. The other girls here are either pearls-and-pursed-lips boarding school types or anorexically cool New York girls.

A drunk guy is shouting in the corner and two girls are whispering near the counter about how in bad taste it is to be so messy in such a nice apartment. Jacob's apartment (really it's his parents' apartment) is on Park Avenue, so we're all expected to behave.

I'm drunk from the vodka that Cameron and I were drinking in the car, but I'm not so drunk that I can't act sober and aloof. The world only seems a little bit sharper and like it's made of richer colors than usual.

I try to float around talking to people but I end up mostly pouring more Coke in my whiskey and Coke to make it seem like I'm busy. Eventually Jacob wanders over to me and leeringly asks me how I'm doing and what it's like living at Lucas'. Him knowing that implies that Lucas talks about me to other people, which I can't imagine him doing.

I'm properly drunk now—vodka always hits me late— and I'm noticing things that I wouldn't normally notice. Lucas' knuckles are scabbed over and the girl Jacob seems to be with has really bad wrinkles at the corners of her eyes.

At this point everyone at the party is drunk, so I end up talking to people I don't know very well. The girls who were talking about how déclassé it was to be messy drunk are dancing in the corner with a scared-looking ginger who I'm pretty sure is a photographer of some sort. He's cross-eyed looking at their boobs and I feel like I want to laugh but I can't laugh. I think about trying to find Cameron to see if he wants to smoke, but he's disappeared.

A blonde girl who was known in high school as "preferring it in the ass" is drinking whiskey and Coke with me. She's very beautiful but her skin is tinged grey. "That over there," she says to me, "is my ex-boyfriend." It's some hockey player I don't know very well but someone pointed him out to me earlier. He's entwined on the couch with one of the anorexic blonde New York girls. "Rough stuff," I say, and I crush our plastic cups together then pour some of my whiskey and Coke into hers. She scowls and walks away. I watch her ex-boyfriend for a little while longer, and even from a distance I can tell that his eyes contain neither light nor intelligence.

Another vague old acquaintance of mine materializes and offers everyone Marlboro Reds. He grew up in Mexico City and is gesticulating and explaining that everyone he knows has been smoking since they were thirteen. I take a cigarette but I can only smoke half before I start to feel like I might throw up. At some point the blonde girl goes away and Lucas comes back. We start talking about books, for some reason. We never talk about books. He's being very charming, or maybe I just feel that way because I'm not used to boys who know how to read and I kind of forgot Lucas could. At this point we're drinking whiskey out of a bottle that someone procured, probably Lucas, and he calls me a "whiskey chick." I ask him what that means and he just smiles and shakes his head.

People are slowly leaving the party for their apartments or other parties and I don't know where Cameron is and it's like I'm in a strange and bad dream and then Lucas grabs my hand and leads me into the bathroom. Everything is marble or gold or mirrored and there are infinite me's and infinite Lucas'. "Woah," I say, giggling. "Look." I hold my hand up to see the million me's do the same thing. Lucas grabs my wrist and kisses me roughly. It doesn't hurt because I'm drunk and I have a high pain tolerance, but I think he is trying to hurt me a little.

"I always think you're so pretty," he says. "You're prettier than everyone here." He's lying. I'm drunk so I want to believe him and I look at him with bleary eyes. I think I smile a little even though hearing him say nice things like that makes me feel nothing. I like him, I probably love him, but right now I'm so tired and my mouth tastes ashy from the cigarette I smoked out the window.

It's surprising when Lucas shoves me down on the toilet and yanks my jeans down to my knees, but not very. I watch one of the many me's stare up at him, open-mouthed. She looks pathetic. Her cheeks were flushed when she came in but now they're very pale. "I should go," I say.

"We're staying here," Lucas says. "Jacob said we could." I nod. Lucas takes a Juul out of his pants pocket and then he takes off his pants. He offers me the Juul and I take it. The toilet is cold against the back of my bare thighs and I wonder where he got the Juul from. Probably one of the anorexic girls. I hand him back the Juul and then his dick is in my mouth and I'm choking and tearing up. My mind is completely blank, it's never blank, and I wonder if anything changed between him and his girlfriend or if he's just drunk and horny and maybe feels like I owe him something, which I probably do.

"Don't look at me," he says. My hair is wrapped around his hand, the one with the scabby knuckles. "Don't fucking look at me." And I honestly think if I weren't so drunk and afraid of everything that this might be hot. Eventually he uses his grip on my hair to pull me up so that I'm bent over the sink. My hair is falling into my face now and it's sticky with sweat.

I really hate it from behind; I think about this while I look at my purple under-eye bags in the mirror. A crust of mascara is developing below my lower lashes and it makes me regret putting it on. Someone knocks on the bathroom door and Lucas says, "no," sharp and on an exhale, and I can hear the nasally cadences of a girl's whining. She probably has to pee really badly. In the mirror I can see that I'm crying and I can't tell if they're residual tears from the choking or if I'm just crying now. I think I'm not actually a whiskey chick, and if Lucas weren't fucking me and we were better friends I would say that to him.

* * *

After we leave the bathroom we don't really talk the rest of the night, but I'm so drunk that all I can remember in the morning is a horrible vague sense that I've embarrassed myself in a way that I can never come back from.

I pee in Jacob's bathroom and more blood comes out of me than I've ever seen come out of anything before. I get nauseous and put my head between my knees until I feel nothing again.

I stumble out of the bathroom and a few people are smoking a j in the living room, probably people who have been awake all night.

"Hey," Cameron says. I didn't realize he was there but now I can't believe I missed him. "Do you want to head back?"

"Yeah," I say.

He doesn't ask me anything else or look at me in a different way than he normally does.

"Lucas went to D.C.," he says. I don't know why Lucas went to D.C. and I don't feel like asking. Probably for an art thing or to visit a friend or maybe just because he felt like it. Either way it has nothing to do with me or anything about me, which makes me feel tiny and weak and small. My hands are shaking and I feel like the only girl in the room who doesn't have her nails done. I probably am. The other girls in the room are slumped over each other on the couch or puffing cross-eyed on a Juul. I wonder if it's Lucas' Juul. It would be like him to leave it here. He can always get another one.

Normally I'd be worried about how I look to these people, but right now all I can think about is taking a shower and sleeping in white sheets with a white duvet cover. I want to put on Cameron's white t-shirt, the one with the pocket over the left part of the chest that's thin and flimsy and lets you see the hair snaking down in a line through his belly button. And the cleanest pair of white underwear I own. Ones that haven't been period-stained or put in the wash so many times they've turned grey.

"You okay?" Cameron is putting his hand on the concave place between my shoulder blades and pushing me out the door.

I didn't say goodbye to anyone. There was nobody I really needed to say goodbye to.

Lucas

Two years ago in London I was fucking a girl who was famous on the internet. I say was like she's dead, which she probably isn't. Or like she's no longer famous, which is probably true. It was something fashion-related that made her famous, so now she's too old. I wouldn't know because I don't really stay in touch with people. But anyway. She was gorgeous. Perfect hair, long legs, etc. Blonde and very pretty brown eyes, the kind of brown eyes that make you believe brown eyes are better than blue ones. I kind of forget why I'm bringing her up. I think because the thing about her that made her different from everyone else is that she would cry when I fucked her and then pretend like she wasn't crying. Like sometimes there would be these loud wracking sobs that would come out and she would pretend like it was nothing. You okay, you okay, I would say sometimes, and she would just nod and dig her nails into my arms. A few times she broke skin. I've got a lot of scars on my arms but she must not have broken skin that hard because I never scarred from her. I think her name was Daisy but I don't really remember.

Chapter Nine

After the party Cameron gets into bed with me. First, I shower, and while I'm in there I can hear him cleaning up my room a little bit. I think he just puts my clothes in a pile and closes the curtains to prevent the afternoon sun from leaking in, but it's still nice.

When I get out of the shower I ask him if he has a clean shirt. He brings me a purple one with a huge blue fish on the back that I've never seen him wear. I get into bed wearing the fish shirt and nothing else and my hair is still completely soaked because I didn't dry it at all. Cameron smooths it gently along my neck and then I think he wipes his hands on the duvet. I start to cry but I do it silently and while staying still so that he won't be able to tell.

"It's alright," he says. "It's alright." He's still touching my wet hair, now without wiping his hands. I have no idea how long we've been in bed but it feels like my eyes have adjusted and we're in a permanent grey morning, trapped in the hour before the sun comes up on a rainy day. Cameron kisses the curve where the back of my neck meets my shoulder. He does it so gently that at first I think it's his fingers brushing my hair away. "Are you hungry?" he asks. "I'm gonna make us grilled cheese."

I don't say anything and he gets up and I can hear him rattling around the kitchen. I'm not sure that he knows where any of the pots and pans are, but soon enough I hear the wet sizzle of butter and I figure he sorted it out. I feel the tension leave my legs. I realize I was ready to stand up, to help him find a pan.

I lie curled on my side and almost feel good for a moment. It's like being a little kid and hearing your mom making breakfast and knowing nothing can hurt you, because why would it? But I'm an adult now, I'm really an adult, and I'm not supposed to need anyone to take care of me.

When Cameron brings the grilled cheeses back they're charred on one side and undercooked on the other, but mine tastes better than anything I've ever eaten in my life.

"The secret is mayonnaise," he says thickly, and I wonder where he learned that. Probably a girl must have taught him. "Do you...wanna, like, watch TV?" He pulls his laptop out from somewhere and starts clicking at the keys with one hand while he shoves the rest of the grilled cheese in his mouth with the other. I don't know when he brought his laptop in but it feels good to be sitting up in the bed with him, the sides of our arms touching and our feet crossed over each other under the duvet.

We watch some stupid cooking show on the BBC and I lean more of my weight against him until my head is completely on his chest. I can hear his heartbeat and it's very fast. Eventually he turns the show off but we don't move, we stay lying there, looking at the empty space where the screen had been. Cameron smells milky and warm from the grilled cheese and I feel so tired that I'm almost confused about why I am where I am.

"Are you tired?" he asks.

"I'm sorry," I say, then I move closer to him and kiss him and he lets me and we lie like that, entwined, kissing until my arm goes numb, and then I think I must fall asleep because when I wake up he's gone and it's like I dreamt him being so nice to me like that.

Cameron left for the city yesterday after a week of virtually ignoring me and today I decided to get drunk. Once you decide to get drunk it's one of those things that's very easy to self-fulfill. It takes me about half an hour before everything looks sparkling and beautiful. I go out to look at the stars with my head tipped back really far and I breathe loud and the breath gets caught in my throat. If anyone could see me right now I bet I'd look ugly and also insane.

Half an hour after this I throw up and then lie on Lucas' bed debating whether I should take a shower. Part of me feels like I don't deserve a shower but the other part of me knows that's stupid and melodramatic. If Cameron were here, I wouldn't have to get drunk. If Lucas were here, I wouldn't have to get drunk. If anyone were here, just to look at me, not even to do anything else, then I wouldn't have to get drunk. All I'm doing is trying to make sure that my body is real. It is, I know it is because I can feel the duvet cover on Lucas' bed reacting badly to the greasy layer of grit on my skin. But it's not my fault I'm dirty. There's no one here to tell me to take a shower.

Earlier today, when I was walking into town, I saw this woman out with her dog. It was one of those horrible little dogs, the kind that's genetically engineered and when you hold it you can feel its tiny heart beating too fast like it's about to die. The old woman was eating a pain au chocolat from the shitty bakery by the movie theater and the whole thing depressed me so much that I had to sit down for a second. I wanted to tell Lucas about it so badly but I couldn't figure out why. I think I just want to talk to him, maybe so he can explain what happened to me.

He wouldn't care about the dog, or if he cared it would only be in that way he cares about what I'm saying right before he tries to have sex with me. It's impossible to make people understand what you're thinking when all anyone ever wants to do is fuck you. I don't understand why it's like this with girls and not boys. Boys seem to have no problem talking about whatever dumb shit it is they're always talking about.

I wish I could see Lucas as a sex object, but I can't, or at least I can't reduce him to that. I remember everything he says, even the stupid, throwaway things, because I listen and because I want to know him.

I end up calling Nell and leaving her a mangled voice-mail where all I say is that the Hamptons are melting my brain call me back. She doesn't call me back and I don't think I've talked to a girl since that party in the city. And that's been the only time since I moved to Lucas', except for Georgia. But she was a robot, not a girl. The closest thing to a girl that I have is Cameron, who left me here for an entire week to go do whatever the fuck it is he does.

My mom is coming tomorrow and I won't be alone anymore. For lunch, at least. I fall asleep thinking about how I hate being alone but also I love it and if you hate anything that much it means you love it.

* * *

My mom takes the ferry and I pick her up at Port Jeff in Lucas' Mini Cooper. She looks wide-eyed and wired, like an unaccompanied minor flying on a plane for the first time. I wonder how much coffee she's had so far today.

When I get out of the car (she demands to drive) she immediately tells me I look like a hooker. I'm wearing a skirt and a tank top with a leather jacket thrown over it. I picked the outfit thinking that it would impress her, or at least that she would take it as a sign that I'm doing mentally well enough to coordinate colors.

"Thanks," I say. I'd tell her to go fuck herself but then she would say that I'm too sensitive and can't take a joke and also she's been here for thirty seconds and I at least want to make it to lunch before we start on each other. I tell her we can get lunch anywhere she wants and she tells me that I can pick. I tell her that I'll eat anything but that most of the food near Lucas' place is shit. She says to not use that kind of language and that we should go to Sag Harbor, which is where she bought my christening dress when I was a baby. "Oh," I say. "Okay. I didn't know that." I have no idea why my mom would have ever gone to Sag Harbor, but I guess it was like a million years ago. I like Sag Harbor even though it's still full of the malevolently rich. There's a good ice cream place there. And the Levain is on the way out. The girls who work at the Levain are cunts, though, and it's almost not worth the cookies.

"So," my mom says, tapping her manicured nails on the steering wheel, "how is everything?" She gets manicures with clear nail polish so that her nails look clean without it seeming like she's a fun person who enjoys colors or frivolity.

"Fine," I say. "I've been writing a lot."

"What have you been writing about?"

"I don't know," I say. My mom always tells me that I should write something like Stephen King would write, with murder. Or historical fiction. But I tell her real life isn't like that at all, not usually anyway. "I write about what I'm thinking about."

"You think there's a market for that?" she asks, and then lets out a clipped, bark-like laugh, the same laugh she does when someone she doesn't like on *Survivor* gets voted off.

My mom makes me very hateful and it's already happening. My knuckles are turning white from where I'm gripping the sides of the seat. It's all very cliché, like a Russian novel without the forbidden romance or the tuberculosis. I'm sure there's a psychological explanation for it that removes all the blame from me as a person. The Electra complex, probably. I do love my dad, even though I never really see him or talk to him.

"Mexican food," I say when I know we're near a burrito place that I know is good. "Let's get Mexican food."

"But don't you eat Mexican food all the time?"

"Yeah," I say. "That's because I like it."

"You're in a bad mood today," she says.

"I didn't sleep well."

"You have to sleep enough." She frowns at me and I can see the deep grooves of her wrinkles. I never want to get wrinkles like that.

It's sunny but cold today and my leather jacket (Lucas' leather jacket) is not warm enough. We're sitting at an outside table in a shady garden and I lean longingly into the single buttery shaft of sunlight that illuminates part of the wooden table. I'm cold and I want to be warm.

We order burritos and my mom complains about how expensive they are. All I can think about is how hungry I am and I accidentally snap, "it's the Hamptons," which makes my mom smile in that way she does when she knows she can criticize me for being a bitch.

"Don't be rude," she says, crossing one thick leg over the other. "I paid."

"I know you paid," I say. I don't say that it's Dad's money anyway and that we all really own nothing.

The burrito I got has potatoes in it and I think about how I'm consuming more carbohydrates in this five-minute span than I have in the past week. It tastes better than it should, and I think it's because my mom got one of those salad-y bowl things and keeps shooting daggers at my burrito. I look at the strip of stomach that's visible between my top and skirt. To me it looks like a roll of fat, but to my mom I'm sure it looks like a golden expanse of youth and freedom. The only time I feel skinny is when I'm around people fatter than me; the only time I feel desirable is around people who obviously aren't, which probably makes me a bad person. But if I am a bad person then it's all my parents' fault.

"Are you coming home for Thanksgiving?" my mom asks. Her salad bowl is empty except for a smudge of guacamole. I tell her I'll think about it. "I really think you should come home," she says. I say I might have a meeting in New York. She asks who the meeting is with and I start babbling about turning my novel into a movie even though I don't even have a novel and even if I did no one would ever want to turn it into a movie.

"That all sounds very exciting," she says. "But wouldn't those kinds of places be closed on Thanksgiving?"

"It's networking, Mom," I say. "I need to be in the city for networking." She says nothing and frowns at her phone. She uses one of those wallet phone cases and I can see the credit cards and cash bursting out of the pockets. I don't understand why she doesn't just get a normal wallet. "You always tell me you want me to have a career."

"There's no need to be accusatory."

"I'm not being accusatory."

"Don't raise your voice." I wasn't raising my voice, but

now she is, and I can see two blonde teenage girls giggling behind their phones. At us, I'm sure. Their arms are covered in those chunky beaded bracelets that are very trendy right now and make everyone look like an eight-year-old who just got back from summer camp.

I'm starting to feel sick, like I want to go to the bathroom and get rid of the burrito I just ate. I can taste onion from the guacamole in my wet mouth and I can see white crust at the corners of my mom's lips.

"I'm sorry," I say. Under the table I switch the cross of my legs and I can feel my rubbery lardy thighs rub against each other. When I'm my mom's age I'll be fat and people like Lucas will have twenty-year-old girlfriends. Every day more girls turn eighteen, nineteen, twenty; every day I get older.

Mom wants dessert, she always wants dessert, and now that things have calmed down I feel guilty and I resent feeling guilty. I always feel guilty even when I haven't done anything wrong. And I haven't, really. Done anything wrong. Maybe I was a bitch to my mom but that's only because she was a bitch to me, like she always is. I can't ever do anything fucking right with her and it's her fault that everything happened the way it happened with Lucas, I know it is.

We leave the burrito garden and I get the sense, like I always do, that I'll never come back here, even though I wouldn't mind coming back.

Mom drives to downtown Sag Harbor. I ask if I can play music and she says no, she'll get a headache. We park the car and I can see the unending grey of the ocean from the unending grey of the parking lot.

The Main Street is fairly deserted except for a young, tired-looking couple and an artsy-looking woman draped in bangles and clothes that look like they're meant to seem like they double as an outfit to do yoga in.

There's a trendy donut shop full of Monstera plants, which is apparently exactly what my mom is looking for. I hate Monstera plants and donuts on principle even though these look lovely and delicious. There's a pink one with glitter brushed halfway across it that's meant to make it look like a galactic spray of stars. The flavor name is Galaxy and I wonder what a Galaxy-flavored donut would taste like. Probably Blue Raspberry. For some reason it all starts to depress me, the sparkles and the Monstera plants and the grey outside and the flavor names that have nothing to do with actual food.

"How's Dad?" I ask once my mom pays for the box of six donuts and carries them out onto the sidewalk. You would think since we're so close to the beach that seagulls would try to get our food, but the Hamptons are so fancy that they've somehow eradicated any seagull-related issues. That or global warming.

"He's good," she says, biting into the glazed one. It's shaped like a star instead of a normal donut. "Working very hard."

We sit on a bench right outside the donut shop. The people behind the counter can see us eating and so can everyone who walks by. Six donuts between two people. "I just want to try the coconut one," my mom says, and she cuts it into quarters with the plastic knife they gave her inside.

There's a fudgy chocolate one that for some reason I want even though I know it's going to make me feel sick. I bite into it without cutting it first and the peanut butter ganache in the middle oozes out the sides. A drop of it splatters on my thigh and I scoop it up with my finger and pop it in my mouth. I barely even chew. It's brushed with orange glitter and I think it's supposed to be Halloween-themed even though Halloween is over. Maybe it's Thanksgiving, now. And then it'll be Christmas and then it'll be summer again. I bet it's perfect here in the summer. I bet I'll never know for sure.

"Try the coconut," my mom says. I want the lemon one first and this one I do cut in half. It's dusted with powdered sugar and it's very beautiful and delicate. I take a sick pleasure in cutting it, in ruining it. It's ugly now, and I put it in my mouth without tasting it. "Good, right?" says my mom. Her eyes are more glazed than the donuts; she's not even looking in the direction of the sea. I wonder if she remembers what it's like to be young.

"Yeah," I say. "Really good."

When I drop my mom off at the ferry she tells me she loves me and she's glad I'm doing well. I drive the Mini Cooper back to Lucas' and then I throw up and my vomit has donut glitter in it.

<h1 style="text-align:center">Cameron</h1>

Friend in the city wants me to house sit. I say I'll probably kill whatever's there. He says nothing's there, I should just go and try to open the windows a few times a day—his parents don't like the feeling that no one's been in the house for months. They say the place gets a weird smell. Okay, sure, I should probably get away from her anyway, after everything that's happened.

I only leave the place to go to the grocery store. I make grilled cheese, quesadillas. I smoke on the fire escape, lie on the couch, the floor. I drink whatever's in the wine fridge. Sometimes, I wonder what she's doing, whether she's okay.

Usually I do a pretty good job of not wondering anything at all.

Chapter Ten

"I'm in Paris," Lucas says. "And I want you to come."

"What?" For a second I think I might be dreaming but my head hurts and in a dream it wouldn't.

"I'm in Paris," he says again, but this time his voice cracks a little bit when he says Paris. "I'm in Paris. Cameron's here too."

"What?"

"You should come," he says. In the background I hear running water and I wonder if it's Lucas' girlfriend or some random girl or if it's just Cameron brushing his teeth.

I almost say what again but then I remember to not be dumb and goldfishy. Instead I say "okay" and think about how I'm going to scrounge up the funds.

"I'll get you a ticket," Lucas says. I wonder if he's on drugs right now. Certainly he is. It's one in the morning here which means it's probably six in Paris. Maybe seven. "Okay," he says. "Bye." I hear the beeping that means he's hung up and then my ears ring in the silence.

Outside the bedroom window the moon glows off dewdrops and I wonder if maybe it rained earlier.

When I wake up in the morning there's an email at the top of my inbox with the subject line Prepare For Your Upcoming Trip to Paris. Three nights: JFK to CDG and back again.

* * *

I'm bored and anxious while I wait to get off the plane so I text my family friend who studies at the Sorbonne and lives in a tiny apartment in the Marais. I entertain the idea of ignoring Lucas and Cameron, of waiting to see them until tomorrow. My friend Ainsley grew up in New York City and once tried to get me to come with her to 1OAK when we were like thirteen. I remember the club promoter met us outside the restaurant we were at and everything. It was probably 2012 and I had never been more terrified by anything in my life. I didn't even go. I left her alone with the promoter. We're friendly now, though. She studies German expressionist cinema and speaks in that nasally rich-girl drawl that I always find so charming.

> I'm not here in Berlin til tmrw
>
> research trip lmao
>
> stay in the apartment tn if u want tho keys
> r in the letterbox xx

I stare at my phone and contemplate the fact that if I want to I can stay in the Marais. For a second I feel like I'm probably not much better than Lucas; I'm just shyer and a girl. Otherwise there would be nothing stopping me from doing what I wanted all the time. But it's not like that, not really.

The first thing I do after I get off the plane is text Lucas asking where he is. Of course he doesn't reply right away; he never does. He's probably sleeping. I could text Cameron, but I know he wouldn't reply either. And he's not the one who invited me here, who owns my time here.

Charles de Gaulle is a nice airport, all white marble and Dior is duty-free. I smile at the glowing Natalie Portmans and Keira Knightleys and the nameless parade of models in perfume advertisements. I thought Parisians didn't wear perfume because they're all disgusting and into pheromones and not showering. But I guess the duty-free isn't geared toward Parisians; it's geared toward rich tourists.

I'm seized by a manic impulse to buy a carton of American Spirits even though I don't really smoke. I stop myself and instead buy a pack of gum and Peanut M&M's. I eat them in an Uber to the Île Saint-Louis because this is where Lucas is staying. When I get out of the car I walk around for a little bit and the air smells like desserts. All the buildings have the same kind of details as a wedding cake and it really is like they're made of frosting because as I stare at them I get terrible stomach cramps. But that's probably just from the plane. Never in my life have I been anywhere this beautiful, not pretty or picturesque or any of those kinds of words, but truly beautiful. I don't understand how so many of the buildings are this perfect, unmarked cream color. I would think that exhaust from the cars and ambient smog would turn them grey, but they're a brilliant radiant creamy white like they're brand new even though it's Europe and everything is old. Even I feel old.

I pass a fancy grocery store and then an ice cream place. I double back to the fancy grocery store and buy an orange, some olives, and a chia pudding. After I pay, I check my phone, and Lucas still hasn't texted me back. I guess I could call him. Or I could get my nails done. It doesn't matter. I'm in Paris because I felt like coming and what kind of girl turns down a free trip to Paris. It had nothing to do with the boys.

I don't think I'll be able to get acrylic nails on the Île Saint-Louis because it's way too old money and it's a tiny little island, so I pull up the map in my phone and walk toward the second, where I assume they'll have the kind of place I'm looking for.

I walk into the darkest, sex-trafficking-frontiest place that I can find. The windows are warped with grime but inside I can see a few tired-looking blonde women whispering while their feet stew in the pedicure soup. The woman at the desk says, "Bonjour," as I walk in and I realize that it's barely even afternoon. I'm definitely jetlagged. I can almost feel my eye bags pulling my face down.

"Quelle couleur?" Her eyes are a deep blue that almost looks purple. They're beautiful, though nothing else about her is. I imagine Lucas violently fucking some girl with eyes exactly like these but with a prettier face, a better body. Then I feel cruel. "Jaune," I say, pointing to a buttery yellow that for some reason looks to me to be very French.

"Vous êtes sûre?" she asks, and when I stare at her blankly, she repeats in English, "are you sure? Your...skin tone." She pronounces skin like skeen and wrinkles her nose when she looks at me.

"Que est-ce que vous pensez?" I say, gesturing at the wall of color.

"Rose," she says. "très très jolie." I stare at the wall for a long time, until the colors all start to melt into each other.

"Bleu," I say, then "bleu clair," because I'm not sure if bleu bébé will translate. She plucks a blue that's too powdery, but at this point I don't really care.

"Oui, Madame," she says, then leads me to a swivel chair that has duct tape covering the cracked white pleather. I'm almost afraid that it'll break when I sit in it, but it just makes a muffled shrieking noise.

A Chinese woman is waiting to do my nails, and she

smiles when I sit. I smile pleasantly back at her. She says something in rapid Chinese to another woman who passes behind her and I wonder if it's about me, then register that this is narcissistic.

The hum of the little machine that files is very soothing. I hear another hum, the buzz of my phone, and I wonder whether it's Lucas texting me back. I find that I don't care but also my shoulders are tensing. I watch my nails turn to dust and then the nail tech takes out a little brush and flicks all the dust away.

When it's over I have beautiful powder blue nails that almost perfectly match the color of the afternoon sky. I got the medium round shape because I couldn't really communicate—my French is limited to schoolgirl phrases and things I remember from movies—but I like how delicate and girlish they make me look. I know Lucas will think they're trashy but I don't care. He can think I'm trashy. To him I'll always be trash no matter what I look like.

The air in this part of town smells like desserts still but also like hot piss. I prefer it to the pure sugary smell. I check Lucas' texts and they're so bizarre that it takes me about three minutes to figure out what he's trying to say.

gettind dinner spon

*soon

come

Then, twenty minutes later:

way

*way

meer here

Then he drops me a pin to some restaurant in the sixth. I call a car, and when I get there I walk around the block because I feel like I can't quite breathe and that I'm maybe too early. It occurs to me that I've never been to Paris before except through books. For a second I want to cry because I wish I could go back in time and come to Paris for the first time with my parents or in a vague future where I'm here with someone who loves me. But I guess like this is just as romantic, in a different way.

I think about buying cigarettes but decide not to. I'm already edgy enough that my hands are shaking. The place Lucas is at looks nice and I'm sure someone will have cigarettes. Lucas usually does.

I give the host Lucas' name and he has no idea where he's sitting so I say I'll look. They don't look like they want me to do that, but I flash a toothy smile and brush past them. The nails are already giving me strength and I feel more like a girl than I ever have.

I see Lucas, finally, through the glass. The black bar of the windowpane obscures his forehead as he sits on the terrace eating steak tartare. Actually it's more like the two guys Lucas is with are eating steak tartare and drinking martinis and Lucas is necking a light beer that looks like Peroni. While I'm looking at him I feel a jabbing pain in my abdomen.

Through the window, I can imagine that he is a stranger, someone I have never met. I would still want him. I think about what his hands feel like, and I can't remember if I'm imagining his hands or someone else's. I wonder where Cameron is, if he's even here. He's not at the table. Lucas takes another sip of his beer. For such a fancy restaurant I'm surprised they serve Peroni.

Walking in I was self-conscious about my outfit (torn baggy jeans, my mom's sheer vintage top, a sweater draped over my shoulders), but Lucas is wearing his usual ill-fitting light wash jeans/t-shirt riddled with holes combo. One of his friends is in a jacket and the other one is in Supreme. It's all very Eurotrash. So, I fit in enough. Lucas and the Supreme friend are shoulder to shoulder in the booth and the suit jacket friend is sitting in one of the fancy little chairs. I toss myself into the other one in a manner that I hope is graceful. Unfortunately the chairs are very close together and most of my body rubs against suit jacket's upper arm. At least he has the decorum not to seem uncomfortable.

"This," Lucas says, "is my really close friend." If we're such close friends then I don't understand why he didn't pull a chair out for me or acknowledge my presence with something other than his usual snarly Patrick Bateman smile.

"What's up," says one of the guys, the one I'm squeezed next to. He's South Asian and when he tells me his name I'm pretty sure Lucas has told me about him before. I thought they hated each other. No one offers to shake my hand but I guess that's normal for young people.

"We'll get you a drink," says Lucas, and Supreme guy finally looks up from his phone to stare at my tits. They do look good in this top, to be fair, but he's eyeing them in the exact same way that suit jacket is looking at the steak tartare.

When the waiter comes back Lucas gestures at me and orders something in rapid French. When the waiter leaves I smile at Lucas through my lashes but he won't hold eye contact with me.

"We're going to Silencio after this," Supreme says. Then he looks at Lucas and asks, "is she coming?" and only now does Lucas look at me.

"Yeah."

I can't decide whether Lucas is more ashamed of me or his friends. Probably me. The boys are sullen and on their phones and I wonder whether it's because of me or because of comedowns or both. Their martini glasses are empty.

The waiter returns with a tray of purple drinks and green shots. The color combination makes me think of *Scooby-Doo* which makes me feel like Velma. Daphne would never be in a situation like this. "Are you hungry?" Lucas asks after everyone drains their drinks in silence. He doesn't sound like he really wants to know either way. I shake my head no, and he gives me a wolfish smile and almost, for a second, looks like he's going to reach out and brush a piece of hair behind my ear.

No one's eating, everyone's just drinking, and it doesn't take very long for me to start feeling sticky and slow. Lucas looks beautiful to me now in the fading pink light. I can forget everything bad he's ever done. I feel like I love him even though I know I don't.

At one point the boys all go to the bathroom to do drugs and Lucas comes back first walking quickly and with giant-floating-saucer-pupils. He sits next to me in the chair instead of going back to the booth.

"I'm, uh, embarrassed," he says. "By my friends."

"I thought you said Cameron was here."

"What?" He shakes his head and breaks eye contact with me. Normally his eye contact is icy and unflinching. When he looks away I suddenly feel very drunk and cold. I think about telling him that I'm cold but I don't want him to think I'm asking for his jacket.

"You're right," I say. "I don't really like your friends." I take a sip of the almost-empty drink that's in front of me even though I'm already extremely drunk and not even sure that the drink is mine. "They're not very nice."

He laughs but still won't look at me. "They're really

alright," he says, drumming his fingers against the white-tableclothed lip of the table. There isn't a single mark on the whole thing. "They're just...they're being bad right now."

"No," I say. "You're right. They're really alright." This isn't what I really think but I feel compelled to say anything to get Lucas to look at me.

"Yeah," Lucas says.

I wonder why I got on a plane and flew for eight hours to come see someone who won't even ask me how the flight was. Part of me is wondering if he even remembers inviting me.

I feel a headache coming on and I would drink water but the only things on the table are what I have ultimately determined are just purple martinis and something else that resembles a gin fizz but is much sweeter and a lurid green color. I have no idea where they came from, or why I keep drinking them.

While I'm pantingly looking around for a waiter who I can beg for water Lucas' friends come back with their eyes gleaming. They're still looking at me like I'm a piece of meat and they haven't had dinner, which I guess I am and they haven't, not really.

I think about speaking but I don't have anything to say so I drink quietly and let the liquid evaporate from my lips. I can feel their eyes on me even when I look out over the terrace to watch the sky bleed.

Lucas still won't look at me and I can't stop digging my sharp new nails into my thigh meat. It occurs to me that Paris is basically the same as New York except it's a little prettier. This restaurant with its blandly fancy décor and neon drinks could be in London or Madrid or anywhere in the entire world, really. I think that's what rich people like so much: the way you can go anywhere in the world and still feel like you're always in the same place. I bet it would make everything less lonely. But right now I feel very lonely.

* * *

At Silencio everything is dark and gold and mirrored in a way that is very cheesy but not in a bad way. There are lots of Eastern European men in tracksuits with gold chains. One of them is handing a handle of Grey Goose to a shiny-haired girl in a Sonic the Hedgehog graphic t-shirt. She has pouty bee-stung lips that are contorted into a grimace. When she sees me looking at her she whispers something to the man in the tracksuit and they both laugh.

I'm not really a club girl but I can appreciate the sultry grittiness of a place like this. Lucas looks good silhouetted against the black and gold of the bar; he looks less pale and unhealthy. But club lighting makes everyone look good. We wait a long time to get drinks and one of the boys, not Lucas, hands me something fizzy and lemony. He asks me if I like it and I say yes even though I can't taste it after the first sip.

"Really good," I say into his neck, right below his ear. This is something I know how to do. "So good." Lucas is still talking to the bartender and his friend who is not him says something else into my ear wetly. I can't hear what it is but I nod and throw back my head to give a charming laugh. He starts laughing too and then I'm dancing in the haze and my whole body feels like it's wrapped in silk.

"This is so fun," I scream to the boy who I'm pretty sure is Lucas' friend. He grins back at me and then hands me his drink. Mine is gone now so I take his and I know how sick I'm going to feel later but I don't care, nothing could be worse than losing this cocoon of numbness, and Lucas isn't anywhere on the dance floor and I don't know why he wanted me to fly halfway around the world if he was just going to ignore me. I think some part of me thought he was going to apologize. I guess, in his way, he did.

The pink light and the body smells are too much for me now and I say, "sorry," to the boy I'm dancing with but I'm quiet enough that he won't be able to hear me.

In the bathroom it's still dark and every single girl is blonde. They give off their own light and I don't know how they're doing it. They all have big eyes and speak European languages and none of them will look at me. I look at myself in the mirror just so I can confirm that I'm not invisible. Underneath my eyes are bruises and they make me look ugly. I am ugly. I'm so ugly. But also I look fine, I'm beautiful, I'm wanted and I'm pretty and perfect and I wish I were really invisible, or I don't, I don't know what I want.

"Do you have lipstick?" asks a blonde girl. I think she's German because she says it like leepsteeck, and I shake my head and look away from the mirror because she's looking at me, her purple-blue eyes are looking at my eyes. "You are pretty," she says, stumbling over to a bathroom stall where she either does nose drugs or throws up—I can't hear which over the dull buzzing in my head.

When I get out of the bathroom the boys are in a booth and there are a few girls with them, all blonde. One of them, I eventually gather, is named Cassie. Someone hands me a drink and I don't know what it is but it tastes like bubblegum. Cassie has straight white teeth and is wearing a pink dress. Her makeup is done in the sixties doll-like way where there are little black lines under the waterline to make her lashes look longer. She is talking to Lucas in a mix of rapid French and perfect English but he isn't looking at her, he's rolling a cigarette and staring at a puddle of spilled drink on the table. I look at the spilled drink too and I see something floating in it, probably a piece of paper from a straw wrapper. Everyone is talking and I can't hear what they're talking about but I don't care. I manage to catch Lucas' eye and I mime smoking a cigarette and he nods. I slide out of the booth and we walk outside to where the air is clear and cool. There are other people around but no one is paying attention to us.

"I'm glad you're here," Lucas says, rolling his cigarette. He doesn't look at me until he licks the paper.

"Me too," I say. "I'm glad I came." I look up at the sky and I can't see the moon right now but I know it's full; I saw it against the dusty blue sky right before the sun set over the restaurant. I'm so drunk that for a second I feel like crying but then I don't. I just look at Lucas with my mouth slightly open, thinking about how if things were different he would kiss me.

We smoke in silence and I can hear the faint vibrations from the thudding techno music inside. It's hard to hold the cigarette with my nails but I manage. Lucas' gaze slides over everything while he smokes. It's very cool outside and the smoke mixes with our breath and makes a thin layer of fog that separates us from the world. I wouldn't mind if it were really like that. Just the two of us alone in Paris.

He hands the cigarette to me and while I smoke he grabs my hand. "When'd you do your nails like this?" he smiles. His grip on my hand is hard enough that it hurts. I can feel the bones in my fingers crunching past the ones in my knuckles.

"Last week," I say. I don't know why I lie. Lucas makes me feel like I can't say what I'm feeling because then he'll use it against me. I'm probably right not to trust him. He smiles and raises his eyebrows and I can tell he likes my nails and also that he's thinking about having sex with me.

"I'm going to go," I say. Lucas' massive pupils eat up his ice blue irises. He blinks at me. "I...just...I'll stay the night in the Marais, because, um, when I wake up...I might want to work." He blinks again. "But you can come with me," I say.

"Okay." He nods and does not break eye contact. "Let me just say bye to the boys." We walk back into the club and he inhales like he's about to say something to me, and then his friend whose suit jacket is now gone materializes from nowhere and says, "Lucas, Cassie found some," and I see the light flash into Lucas' eyes for a second and he says, "oh, okay," and then looks at me and we don't have to say anything more because I know it's over.

"Bye." I whisper it into his ear but I know my warm breath on his neck does nothing for him, not right now.

And tonight I don't feel like being the girl who hangs around until he's ready to take me home. I've done it so many times before and I'm tired and I don't want to do drugs.

I walk home alone and cry and feel sorry for myself. I don't care if he's going to fuck Cassie, if the suit jacket guy is going to fuck Cassie, if they're all going to gang-rape Cassie. I don't care and I'll never know.

I shouldn't have come. But I was always going to. I don't feel like I exist unless someone like Lucas is watching me. The streets are still pretty in the dark but I'm not really paying attention to them.

When I open my friend's apartment a Margiela blazer is hanging from one of the closet doors. It's like it glowers at me, mocks me for being in cheap jeans. She has a train schedule and pictures of friends hanging from the refrigerator. All of them are stuck with funky magnets that I imagine were gifts from her friends, the ones in the pictures smiling and holding drinks and wearing plastic sunglasses.

I fall into bed and don't wash my face or take my clothes off or even get under the covers. I lie there half-asleep all night, my eyes glued to the ceiling, thinking about how no matter where I am in the world it's always going to be like this.

* * *

When she's back from Berlin Ainsley meets me in Montmartre. I've been wandering aimlessly all day trying to see some of the city while I'm still here. The only thing I did was go into Sainte-Chapelle and the light streaming through the stained glass looked like ropes of candy, the kind you eat when you're a little kid. It was so beautiful in there that I got upset because I knew I might not ever see anything that beautiful again in my life. But now it's evening and I'm looking at a crusted piece of McDonald's McFlurry dripping down the side of a trash can.

"Oh my God, hey," she drawls, drawing out all the vowels so that the sentence takes ages to pour out of her mouth. "Why do you have your bag?" Her little dachshund that I forgot she had is yelping and attempting to scrabble up my bare legs. I can see angry little red marks forming from where her stubby paws meet my skin. "Albie, *down*," she hisses. The dog is named Albie which is short for Albondiga which means meatball in Spanish, a language I'm relatively sure Ainsley doesn't speak.

"I'm going home tonight," I say. "I changed my flight."

"Oh, what," she says. She crouches down to smooth Albie's quivering head. "Why?"

I don't feel like launching into the well-I-have-this-friend-whose-house-I-live-in explainer so I just say, "gotta get back to New York," and she nods.

"I met this guy on Raya," she says. She adjusts the claw clip in her hair and it looks worse than it did before she touched it. "Who you'd die for."

"Show me him," I say, and she does, and he's hot, and I

146

do die for him a little bit, and I guess it's good to know that there's a part of me that's still alive. She tells me he's a skateboarder and that the sex is good but not amazing, but that it's easier to sleep with someone you already know than to constantly be looking for new people to sleep with. I catch a glimpse of her profile photo before she closes out the app, and she looks unrecognizably beautiful in it. I've never been one of those girls who looks different in photos or with makeup, and I imagine it would be disorienting for her sense of self. But what do I know? I'm probably just jealous of her and her rich people dating app and her nice things.

I notice we're walking past an expensive boutique that I think we've already walked past before. There's a headless mannequin in the window draped in shawls and she's stretching out an arm the way people do when they're ironically asking you for a dance.

"You hungry?" Ainsley drawls, and I notice that I am. I haven't eaten much in Paris, the food capital of the entire fucking world. We're close to a carousel with a bunch of little kids shrieking and running around and it occurs to me that French children even shriek and run around more politely than American ones.

We go into a bakery near the carousel that she says is supposed to be very good. Everything is glistening and covered in powdered sugar. A small French boy on a scooter is pointing excitedly at an almond croissant. I smile at the boy and he hides behind his father's legs. The father leers at us and then I order a pistachio-apricot tart. Ainsley gets something with cream and strawberries and hands the bakery girl a handful of bills and coins.

We sit on a bench by the carousel and eat quietly. The tart is maybe better than anything I've ever tasted, and when I close my eyes for a second I feel lucky to be here, to be alive. But when I open my eyes I see the faded, chipped blue paint on one of the carousel horses and the feeling goes away. I wipe crumbs away from my mouth and ask Ainsley if she wants the rest of my tart. She's already finished eating hers. She waves the tart away so I slowly finish eating it even though it doesn't taste good anymore. Near our bench a little boy, a different one from inside the bakery, falls off a scooter and skins his knee. He cries quietly and I watch his mother pat his head gently to comfort him.

"You've seen Sacré-Cœur, right?" Ainsley jabs away at her phone, probably replying to the skateboarder's Instagram DM.

I shake my head, but she's not looking at me. "No," I say. A different friend of mine told me that you can stay with the nuns at Sacre-Cœur. Probably not such a bad deal if you're broke or just really into waking up at three in the morning to pray. If I come back to Paris, that's where I'll stay.

"Oh," she says. "We should go. We're right by there."

I nod and we get up. On the walk there are blankets of leaves and patches of dying flowers and ones that are still alive. Ainsley talks about an old man that she had sex with. She said it took him almost half an hour of eating her out to get hard, and then when they finally did have sex he didn't finish. He took her out to a bunch of fancy dinners but she says they only slept together three times.

"Did you like him?" I ask, and she laughs.

"Yeah," she says. "He was nice." Her tone of voice makes it impossible for me to know whether she's telling the truth. She says she's been smoking a ton of Parisian hash and swiping on Tinder and I wonder when she has time to do her very important schoolwork.

We walk into Sacre-Cœur and there's a few people wandering around and a woman in all black quietly praying. I walk toward the back and leave Ainsley to check her DMs.

She's an atheist so I don't think this is a sacred space for her in the way it is for me, a good Catholic girl.

Near the pulpit there's a statue of Jesus in what looks like solid silver, one hand pressed to his heart and the other hand upturned. I read the description tag and find out that the statue is, in fact, solid silver. I wonder how much someone has to love Jesus to make a statue like that and whether, in making it, they start to hate him a little bit. Either way I can't look at it for too long because the flat orbs of blank silver that would be his eyes are scaring me. They look very sad.

Ainsley comes up behind me. "AFC," she whispers.

"What?"

"Another fucking church." I turn around and see her rolling her eyes. Then she walks away and starts examining a painting very intently. I let her be and pray to Jesus and the Virgin Mary to forgive me for having so much premarital sex. I'm sorry, I'm sorry, I'm sorry but also it's not my fault. Something tells me that they do forgive me but also that I'm not done being punished. Maybe this something is just my own unconscious. It's beautiful in Sacre-Cœur but very dark and continental and when I'm done praying I get up and walk by my friend.

"Ready?" I whisper, and she nods. I wonder what it's like being inside a cathedral when you're not Catholic and it freaks me out that I'll never know. I remember realizing a few years ago that I would never know what it's like to have sex as a man, and I felt the exact same way.

When we walk out the sun is pressing through the clouds in golden rays that look shot through with silver. It's starting to set but there's no pink or purple or orange in the sky. This time tomorrow, when the sun sets, I'll be back in the Hamptons, watching the sky change through the massive gaping windows. I wonder if the beautiful sun coming out is God or just the weather. The rays are a light golden, a white gold, and I feel like they must be God. But if they're God then they can't be for me, they must be for someone else, and I look around at the other people on the church steps. Most of them are on their phones. I realize that I'm hungry and I tell Ainsley that I haven't eaten much today. Actually the pistachio-apricot tart is the only thing. She says she knows a good burger place, so I tear my eyes away from the sky and the church and we descend the steps back into Montmartre, back into the city.

We go to a takeaway she knows and eat cheeseburgers dripping in juice under the awning of a clothing store while the sun finishes setting. The dripping juice is the color of blood but I don't care. After I throw the wrappers in the trash she says she loves my nails. I smile and tell her I got them done here.

In my taxi to the airport through the grim outskirts of the city, I stare out the window at the Carrefours and business hotels and think about how easy it would be for Lucas to just lie and tell me he loves me. But maybe it's a good thing that he doesn't. Tell me he loves me, that is. I wish I could be happy and wear Margiela blazers on Raya dates in Paris like Ainsley, whose life seems impossibly glamorous to me. But she's not actually happy, I don't think, and I don't look good in blazers.

* * *

I always get to the airport embarrassingly early, which is something I don't like people to know about me. Much sexier to sprint onto the plane moments before the gates shut. Anyway I was so early that I took one of Lucas' Xanax at the gate and someone had to shake me awake to let me know that the plane was boarding. I took another Xanax right before takeoff and slept almost the entire flight.

Now I'm back in New York and Cameron is waiting to pick me up at JFK in a car I've never seen. Turns out he was here basically the whole time, bumming around the city, and Lucas is just a fucking drug addict and a liar, but these are things I could have guessed if I thought about them.

"How was it?" he asks. I shrug.

"Have you ever seen *Frances Ha*?" I ask. I look out the window at the sky which is a familiar purple here and therefore much more beautiful.

"No," he says.

I say it's a Noah Baumbach movie. He says is that the guy who did *Marriage Story*. I say yes, and we drive in silence for a while and then he turns on the music.

"Are you hungry?" he asks eventually.

"Yes," I say. "I'm starving."

We go to McDonald's and get Big Macs and sodas and we have them on the LIE. I'm so happy I could cry and I just like being here, being home, music playing and it's warm enough to have the windows down, which Cameron lets me do on the highway even though it means we get worse gas mileage.

What I don't say to Cameron is that on the plane back to New York I got my period. It was almost three weeks late and if it had been something it would have been Cameron's something, I'm sure of it.

In the blue glow of the plane bathroom the blood pouring out of me looked completely black, but in the dirty mirror I was smiling. My face was lit up blue and my teeth were white and glowing. I looked like a monster, and I wondered if spending time around Lucas made me as evil as he is. It was probably just the Xanax and nothing more serious and I shoved thin airplane toilet paper into my pants and that was that. No baby. Pas de bébé.

Lucas

A bunch of girls somebody knows from prep school at an apartment in the sixth. They look a little young. Someone has gin. We all drink right out of the bottle. Smoke out the window. The girls giggle about falling. Nobody falls. Someone has coke. The girls are happy. Everyone's happy. It's a great night. One of them follows me into the bathroom. "Are you someone's sister?" I ask her. She shakes her head, gets on her knees in front of me. I can see myself in the mirror, but then I close my eyes.

Chapter Eleven

I wake up next to Cameron even though we didn't have sex. Last night I asked him if I could sleep in his room and he said okay and then he didn't touch me until he fell asleep, when he curled into my back like we were in real love.

"Hi," he says, and his voice is all raspy and croaky and his hair is knotted with morning. In the light from the window it glows like copper, like the French copper pots my grandma used to hang in her kitchen even though she never cooked. "Happy, um, Happy Thanksgiving," he says, and then we both start laughing. On Thanksgiving you're supposed to wake up cocooned in the warm down of your childhood bed while your mom cooks gravy or bacon or something. I probably could even have that, or something resembling it, if I just fucking got on the train and went home. Cameron couldn't, though. He's told me he thinks his parents wish they never had him. He gets that vacant stare in his beetle-black eyes when he smokes weed and I can tell he's thinking about how his family never wants him around. If that were me I'd probably kill myself. But I think the amount your parents want you ends up being pretty inversely proportional to the amount of money they give you, at least in cases like Cameron's. And he gets more than enough money to keep himself alive.

"Why aren't you home?," he asks. I look out the window at the wall of hedges. I think I see someone moving through the gaps in the leaves, but I know it's probably only a bird.

"Go home," I say, too tired to inflect properly even though I mean to be saying it like a question. I turn toward him and smile so he knows I'm delighting him with my dry wit. "Go *home*? And leave paradise?"

He smiles. "We don't have to stay here, you know," he says. He gets up in bed and gropes for something on the nightstand, probably a vape. He brings his hand to his mouth and sucks on the Juul, the baby sucking its thumb even though Cameron's thumbs are big, and then I reach for it.

"Where could we go," I say. "The beach?" It's cold now, cloudy with that thick, slate-grey sky that won't melt into something nicer until March or April, and I don't want to go to the beach.

"My apartment," he says. "Well, my parents' apartment."

"Where are your parents?"

"St. Barthes," he says.

I don't know where St. Barthes is, but I know it's a place that's entirely inaccessible to me.

I wonder what Cameron would do if I asked him to choose between being Lucas' friend and my whatever-he-is-to-me. I guess he would choose Lucas because I have nothing to offer him besides sex, which he said he doesn't want anymore. I'm sure he'll go back on that but I do know that he doesn't want to want it, for some reason. Probably because he thinks I'm trash and he could never really be with somebody like me.

"Alright," I say. He climbs out of bed. I look at the curve of his long back catching the light from the window. I'll miss the light, but I don't think I'll miss anything else.

I hear Cameron brushing his teeth and I take it as a signal to go make Nespressos. I've gotten a lot better at figuring out what men want from me, I think.

* * *

We take Lucas' convertible. I wear a scarf over my hair and it makes me feel like Jackie O.

I don't understand why we're taking Lucas' car or where we're going to put it once we get into the city. I wonder if Cameron knows or asked Lucas about it. I bet he didn't. I don't think he thinks about things the way I do, but boys never do.

I wonder if I should have left Lucas a note or a gift or something for letting me stay. It would have ended up in the trash, I'm sure, and seemed stupid and pathetic to him, but it might have made me feel better.

The road out of the Hamptons is beautiful in an Americana strip-mallish way and it makes me sad. I wonder if I'll ever come back to Lucas' house or to the Hamptons at all. I'd like to think that I will, one day, but I know it's more likely that this is the last I'll ever see of both. We pass the Indian restaurant I always wanted to try but never did, and I imagine what would happen if I said no, stop, turn around, go back, but by then we're already at the flashing neon lights of the tobacco stands near the highway. The sky is a smudged blue-grey and all the colors look more neon and I feel like I could drive in this car with Cameron forever.

"You okay?" he asks, and I nod. He looks away from the

road to look at me and we both start laughing, I don't know why. It feels like I'm starting to understand something that I'll never fully understand.

"Freedom," I say, but I don't think he hears me. We're on the highway now and going so fast that the wind hurts my face. I throw my arm out and let the breeze hold it steady in the air. It's warm for Thanksgiving, the way it always is, football-on-the-lawn-after-pie air, warm and thick.

He turns on the radio and starts playing a Donna Summer song, which is bizarre and makes me laugh. I bounce in my seat and for the first time since the summer I feel like I'm actively having a good time. This is life, I think. This is my life. I don't have to go home for Thanksgiving ever again, not if I don't want to. I don't have to see Lucas ever again. Cameron reaches over and touches my shoulder, and he could be anyone touching me. He just couldn't be no one.

Acknowledgments

Thank you to the following people, without whom this book would not exist:

Leza, Christoph, and everyone at CLASH
John Burnside
Alessandra Thom, who read about a hundred drafts
Matthew McCaffrey
Mom, Dad, and Ryan
Gillian Rothenberg

About the Author

Nicole Sellew is a writer and English teacher living in Connecticut. She received her MLitt from the University of St Andrews in 2022, and is currently studying for her PhD.